OPERATOR 5:
THE ARMY WITHOUT A COUNTRY

SECRET SERVICE OPERATOR #5 ™

AMERICA'S UNDERCOVER ACE

THE ARMY WITHOUT A COUNTRY

By Curtis Steele

POPULAR PUBLICATIONS • 2022

CHAPTER 1
DOOM AT THE DIVIDE

THE TALL crests of the Continental Divide cast a deep, menacing shadow over the rolling Colorado country west of Denver, as the two horsemen anxiously spurred through the night. The hooves of their horses were wrapped in gunnysack so that no slightest noise gave evidence of their progress. The leading horseman was a tall, fair-haired young man in his early thirties. He sat erect, one hand upon the holster of the service revolver at his side, the other holding the reins in an almost feathery grip. His companion, who followed perhaps ten paces behind, was a lad of not more than fifteen or sixteen, freckle-faced, with a pert Irish nose. The boy was dressed in a lumberjacket and riding-breeches, while the man whom he followed wore the trim uniform of a captain of Intelligence of His Majesty Rudolph I, Emperor of the Purple Empire.

A close observer would have noticed that the lad who rode behind this captain was maneuvering his horse with difficulty, due to the fact that his wrists were handcuffed in front of him.

As a matter of fact, while these two rode through the night they were not unobserved, for upon a ridge a half mile to the north a small squad of Purple Empire troopers was standing at attention while the sergeant in command of the detail focused a night-glass upon the horsemen. After carefully observing them

1

for several minutes, the sergeant put down his glass and turned to the troop.

"It is one of our own officers," he grumbled, "and he has a prisoner. But let us ride down and intercept them. It may be an American spy in disguise. These Americans are sending spies over every day now."

The troop mounted at a signal from the sergeant and followed him down a narrow, winding path toward the road below.

"Don't move, Sergeant!" Operator 5's voice cracked.

The stillness of the night carried with it a dread foreboding. Only a few miles to the west two mighty armies lay in their trenches, waiting only the word which would send them at each other's throats in the deciding battle of the Purple invasion.*

* AUTHOR'S NOTE: Those of our readers who have followed the history of the Purple Invasion of America will recall that the powerful, mechanized armies of Rudolph I, Emperor of the Purple Empire, had conquered Europe and

For fourteen months the mighty armies of Rudolph I, Emperor of the Purple Empire, master of Europe and Asia, had driven the woefully unprepared forces of America steadily westward from the Atlantic seaboard. With fire and sword they had devastated the country, setting up the imperial rule of Rudolph in place of our own free government. Now at last America had rallied every man at her command in one last final, desperate attempt to hurl back the ruthless invaders. If our armies should fail at the Continental Divide, then history would no longer record the activities of any free government on the face of the earth. America, the last outpost of democracy, would then be prostrate beneath the iron heel of imperialism.

And this section of Colorado, just east of the Continental Divide, was in enemy territory. The platoon of Purple troopers

Asia, and had then turned their attention to the United States. With recruits taken from every portion of the earth, the Purple Empire had equipped the greatest army ever assembled in the history of the world, and had descended upon our shores. Ruthlessly, our Defense Force was driven back toward the Pacific Coast. The bravery and the self sacrifice of our men could not stand against the steel and the shells of the enemy. At the Continental Divide our Defense Force gathered for one last supreme effort to drive back the enemy. At this time the destruction of America was so complete, that the opposing armies were at last a little more evenly matched. Oil wells, ammunition and armament factories had been destroyed; the two forces were reduced to relatively elemental modes of conflict. Tanks and airplanes were a thing of the past. Primitive man was facing primitive man—in a struggle to the death, and without quarter.

under that sergeant was one of innumerable similar outposts along the entire far-flung battle line from Canada to the Mexican border.

Being on their own territory, the Purple troopers made no effort to conceal their approach toward the two riders on the road below. Their horses' hooves struck sparks from the gravel paths as they rode swiftly toward their goal, and the two riders on the road below could not help but hear them.

THE YOUNG captain, riding slowly in advance of his captive brought his mount to a halt and turned to peer through the night in the direction from which the troopers were coming. Strangely enough, he did not even glance behind him to see if his prisoner were safe. And, even more strangely, he spoke to the young captive in English.

"I think we're spotted, Tim," he said. "Now remember your story and we'll get by. If you slip up, they'll stand us both against a wall."

"Don't worry about me, Jimmy. I'll give them an act that will bring the house down."

"It's not us that we have to worry about, Tim," Jimmy said. "Remember that we've got a job to do tonight. If we don't contact Frank MacPherson tonight, everything is lost. I was hoping he'd send out a detachment of his Arizona Scouts to meet us. It would have simplified matters. Remember, we've got to get through. Everything depends on us!"

The boy rattled his handcuffs. "Do you think they'll notice that these aren't locked?"

The young officer shrugged. "We'll have to take a chance

on that. You can't afford to lock the handcuffs. You might have to get your hands free in a hurry."

The Purple troopers were now less than fifty feet away, and they slowed up while the sergeant rode toward them.

The sergeant pulled up his mount, close to the young officer's, and saluted respectfully.

"Your pardon, my Captain," he said, in the guttural language of the Purple Empire, "but our instructions for tonight are to stop and question everyone who passes."

"That is well, Sergeant," the young captain replied gravely. "I am Captain Von der Getz of the Imperial Intelligence. I am returning from an excursion into the American lines and am bringing back a prisoner. This boy has vital information which must reach Imperial Headquarters without delay, before the impending battle."

The Purple sergeant glanced for the first time at the youthful prisoner who sat his horse quietly behind the captain. Suddenly, the sergeant's eyes opened wide in astonishment.

"*Himmel!*" he exclaimed. He thrust his hand into his tunic and withdrew a small, printed poster about eight by ten. He unfolded this and turned his flashlight upon it. There were two photographs on this poster. The first was that of a young man in civilian clothes, clear-eyed, straight-nosed, with a firm unyielding chin. Beneath the picture was printed in English and in the language of the Purple Empire, the following notice—

THE ARMY WITHOUT A COUNTRY

WANTED DEAD OR ALIVE

His Imperial Highness, Rudolph I, will pay a reward of one hundred pounds of pure gold to any person who will furnish information leading to the capture of James Christopher, otherwise known as Operator 5, whose photograph appears above. Any American civilian residing in Occupied Territory who furnishes the said information will further be excused from all forced labor duty, in addition to the reward. If the information be furnished by a Purple trooper or officer, then that trooper or officer shall, in addition to the reward, be created a baron of the Empire.

Alongside the photograph of Operator 5, there was another picture—a likeness of the handcuffed boy. The text under the boy's photograph read as follows—

WANTED DEAD OR ALIVE

The boy, Tim Donovan, whose photograph appears above, is known to be the constant companion of Operator 5, and will no doubt be found in his company. A reward of fifty pounds of pure gold will be paid for his capture. All Purple troopers and officers are warned to be very careful, as the boy's youth is deceiving. He is almost as expert with a gun as Operator 5, and has already escaped capture on several occasions in the past.

The sergeant stared from the photograph on the poster to the handcuffed boy.

"Himmel!" he exclaimed once more. "My Captain, permit me to congratulate you. You have captured the brat, Tim Donovan."

The young captain of Intelligence twirled his mustache smugly. "It is true. Not only that, but I have induced him to tell us all he knows of Operator 5's plans for the coming battle."

The captain turned sharply and placed a heavy hand on the boy's shoulder. "Is it not so, brat?" he demanded harshly. He shook the boy vigorously, and the lad seemed almost to cringe from him. What the Purple sergeant did not see was the broad wink which the captain gave the boy as he shook him.

Tim Donovan exclaimed, with a good appearance of fear, "Yes, yes, Captain, I'll talk—only don't beat me."

The sergeant laughed harshly. "Hah! So this is that little devil who is supposed to be so brave! You threaten to beat him, and he is ready to talk! Hah!"

THE MOMENTARY distraction had taken the sergeant's attention away from the photograph of Operator 5 beside that of Tim Donovan in the poster. Had it not been for that distraction he might have noticed that there was a startling resemblance between the features of the man whose photograph was labeled *Operator 5* and those of the young captain of Intelligence.

True, the face of Operator 5 in the photograph was clean-shaven, while that of the Intelligence captain sported a small, nattily-trimmed imperial mustache. Also, the Intelligence captain's nose was much broader than that of the man in the photograph. His lips appeared to be much thicker and his cheekbones higher. Of course, the Purple sergeant could not know that the Intelligence captain's nose had been widened by the use of thin, aluminum plates, or that his lips had been made to appear thicker by the use of make-up, and his cheekbones higher by the clever application of plastic material.

Had he been keen enough to notice the resemblance beneath those superficial changes, the sergeant's whole life might have been changed. Had he realized that the man who sat his mount so nonchalantly before him was in truth Jimmy Christopher, otherwise known as Operator 5, arch-enemy of the Purple Emperor, he might that day have risen at one bound from the position of a lowly non-commissioned officer to that of a baron of the Empire.

But Operator 5's adeptness at disguise had often hoodwinked shrewder persons than this sergeant of the Purple Armies. The very boldness of his appearance here, with Tim Donovan in tow was enough to divert suspicion from himself. Now, Operator 5 smiled with all the haughty pride of which officers of the Purple Empire were capable, and said: "You may return to your position on the ridge, Sergeant. I will proceed alone with my prisoner." Tim Donovan, behind him, gripped tightly on the reins of his horse. The one thing they had feared in this nocturnal venture had not yet come to pass—that is, the demand for the password. Operator 5 did not know the password of the day within the Purple lines, and he was counting upon his appearance and the brazenness of his attitude to carry him through without it. The dozen or so troopers behind the sergeant were sitting more or less at their ease upon their mounts, eyeing the pseudo-captain with veiled envy; for they knew that this man would tomorrow be basking in the sunshine of the Imperial favor. Nevertheless, their carbines were unslung, and under their arms ready for use. Should the slightest suspicion arise in the mind of the sergeant, there was little hope that Operator 5 and Tim Donovan could escape.

The sergeant saluted obsequiously, saying, "You may pass, my Captain, with your prisoner."

Jimmy Christopher returned his salute carelessly, and spurred his horse into the road, with Tim Donovan following. Tim kept his handcuffed hands close to the waistband of his breeches, where a revolver rested snugly hidden. His youthful face was furrowed with anxiety. Would the sergeant really forget to demand the password?

He glanced behind, saw that the sergeant was turning to lead his platoon back up the road that led to the top of the ridge.

"Gosh Jimmy," he called softly, "I think we're getting away with it—"

And it was at that moment that the blow fell.

The sergeant, abruptly reigning in his horse called after them, "One moment, my Captain!"

THEY WERE not far away enough to act as if they had not heard. Jimmy Christopher called back to Tim in a sharp, low voice: "Get set, kid. I think we're in for it." He pulled his mount to a halt, and glanced back, frowning. "What is it?" he demanded impatiently of the soldier.

The sergeant motioned to his troopers to remain behind, and spurred his horse toward them.

"I forgot one thing, my Captain. Merely a formality, sir. If you will just give me the password of the day, that will be all."

Jimmy Christopher put all the harshness at his command into his voice. "That is impossible, Sergeant. You must understand that I have been away, inside the enemy lines for forty-eight hours. Therefore, I could not have the password of the day."

The sergeant was now only ten or fifteen paces away from them, and, even in the darkness, Jimmy Christopher noted that the man's hand stole upward toward the holster at his side.

"I am sorry, my Captain, but you know that it is our custom to issue the password for two days in advance. Therefore, you should have it today. I will have to hold you for further questioning by the colonel—"

Jimmy Christopher tried to bluster. "This is ridiculous, Sergeant! I refuse to be detained like this—"

The sergeant shrugged. "That is too bad, my Captain. But orders are orders. It is very strange that you do not have the word."

Jimmy Christopher breathed a deep sigh of resignation. "We have to fight, Tim," he muttered.

His narrowed eyes were focused upon the sergeant's hand, which was slowly drawing the revolver from his holster. With a motion so swift that it was almost imperceptible to the eye, his own hand moved down and up, appearing with his own gun.

"Don't move, Sergeant!" Operator 5's voice cracked through the night.

The sergeant's face went white as he found himself staring into the muzzle of Jimmy Christopher's revolver. His lips drew back from his teeth in a tight snarl.

"You're a spy!" he rapped out. Then he raised his voice in a

11

hoarse shout to his men. "They are spies! Shoot them down!"

At his command, the platoon of troopers became galvanized into action. They raised their carbines, spurring their horses forward. But they could not shoot yet, for the sergeant was squarely in the road between them and the two Americans.

Jimmy Christopher pushed his mount closer toward the sergeant, thrusting his revolver forward so that its muzzle was almost touching the man's stomach. At the same time, he called over his shoulder to Tim Donovan: "Get going, Tim! I'll hold them here. You know where to go and what to do. Don't fail, now!"

Tim Donovan exclaimed: "Nix, Jimmy. I can't leave you like this. I'm sticking—"

"Get going, I say!" Jimmy Christopher's voice rasped with the harshness of a whipsaw.

"No, Jimmy, I won't—"

Operator 5's left arm swung around in a wicked backhanded blow to the flank of Tim Donovan's horse. The animal, startled by the blow, reared up on its hind legs, and then raced madly away down the road with Tim Donovan clinging to it. Operator 5 was left alone to face the sergeant and his platoon of men.

The troopers were almost upon them now, and spreading out

in the road on either side of the sergeant's horse to get at Jimmy Christopher.

Operator 5 bent low in the saddle, seized the reins of the sergeant's horse, and spurred straight forward directly into the path of the charging troopers. The sergeant's mount, urged by Jimmy's hand on the reins, cantered uncertainly alongside of him, protecting his left flank from the troopers.

The Purple Uhlans were momentarily taken aback by his unexpected action. It was a good half minute before their sluggish mental processes adjusted themselves to the emergency. And in those thirty seconds Operator 5 gained twenty yards on them. He swung about in his saddle just in time to strike up the arm of the Purple sergeant, who had succeeded in drawing his revolver. The sergeant's gun exploded harmlessly in the air, and the man, thrown off balance by Jimmy's blow, fell sideways from his horse. His left leg was tangled with the stirrup, and he uttered a single scream as his mount dragged him along the gravel road. His head bounced again and again upon the hard stone, and then he became a silent, inert mass. His horse swerved sharply, dragging him after it.

Jimmy Christopher did not look behind him again. Bending low in the saddle, so that his breath fanned the horse's mane, he urged his mount forward.

CHAPTER 2
ARIZONA TO THE FRONT!

S LUGS FROM the carbines of the Purple troopers began to whine through the air about him. The accident to the sergeant had slowed up the Uhlans for another moment, giving Jimmy Christopher an additional lease on life. The distance between him and the troopers was now great enough to make night shooting fairly uncertain. He, himself, bending low over his mount, afforded a small enough target, but he knew that at any moment his horse would be hit. It was a tight spot.

He was riding far forward in the saddle, like a jockey on a racing horse. Any shot that caused his animal to falter in its stride would send him hurtling over the horse's head into the road. Such a spill, even if it did not kill him, would stun him and result in inevitable capture.

The night had become a pandemonium of barking rifles and hoarse shouts. The Uhlans had entirely forgotten Tim Donovan, and were concentrating upon the chase after the man who had killed their sergeant. This was what Jimmy Christopher had wanted. As he rode recklessly on into the night, with the pursuing Uhlans strung out behind him, thought after thought flashed through his mind with the kaleidoscopic swiftness of a dying man's brain.

He felt a fierce surge of exultation at having gotten Tim Donovan free of the troopers. He and the boy had been riding on an important mission that night. The America G.H.Q. had set tomorrow at six o'clock as zero hour for the big push against the

Imperial troopers in the Continental Divide. And it was Operator 5's mission to consolidate all the civilians in the occupied territory behind the enemy lines into the unified uprising which should take place simultaneously with the big drive.

Tim Donovan knew his plans, and could carry them out as well as he, and all the Americans in the occupied territory knew that the boy enjoyed Operator 5's fullest confidence. Jimmy Christopher had picked up the lad, Tim Donovan, in the streets of New York. The boy was at that time able to render him a signal service, and ever since then Operator 5 had taken the lad under his wing. He had taught him to shoot as well as a grown man, to ride a horse, drive an automobile, pilot an airplane, send and take Morse code—so that the freckle-faced Irish boy was as efficient an assistant as any grown man could have been. In the days before the Purple Invasion, when Operator 5 was the chief operative of the United States Intelligence, the boy had nursed ambitions of one time becoming an Intelligence Operative, himself. Now, however, the one thought in the mind of Tim Donovan, of Operator 5, and of every other red-blooded American was to drive the ruthless Imperial Purple Conqueror from our shores and to make America once more a free nation.

When Jimmy Christopher struck the flank of Tim Donovan's horse, he had acted impetuously, on the spur of the moment, without giving thought to anything but the fact that he wanted the boy to be safe. And now, as he rode hard, bent low over his horse, with the carbines of the enemy troopers whining past him, he was glad that Tim Donovan was out of danger.

The Uhlans behind him were yelling like madmen, roweling

their horses' sides cruelly with their spurs in an attempt to cut the distance between them and their quarry.

The drumming of the horses' hooves echoed back from mountain walls to the west like the ominous beat of a dead march. Jimmy Christopher, straining his eyes to pierce through the darkness ahead, could see no hope of escape. His lips were set in a thin, tight line; his eyes were bleak, hard. He had lived through many dangers, and escaped from many perils in the past, but he had always faced them fighting—never running. The only upshot of this chase could be a bullet in the back, or, if he were thrown from his horse and captured, a far worse fate. For Emperor Rudolf had promised him a painful and lingering death.

A BULLET tugged at his coat, another creased his left shoulder. The shots were coming closer now. As the Uhlans settled down to the chase, they were shooting with greater accuracy. It would be only a matter of seconds before they struck him or his horse.

Jimmy Christopher laughed harshly. In that laughter there was a touch of gay bravado, fatalistic bravery. Jimmy Christopher did not intend, if he could help it, ever to be found with a bullet in his back. If he had to die, he wanted to meet his death face to face. And through his head, as he urged his horse to the limit, there drummed the words that a famous poet put into the mouth of a great and famous soldier—

> To every man upon this earth
> Death cometh soon or late

16

And how can man die better
Than facing fearful odds
For the ashes of his fathers
And the temples of his gods!

Jimmy Christopher was as ready to die for his country as was Horatius in the brave days of old. He regretted only that he could not live to see his country once more free. If his hour had come he would give a good account of himself. The rattle of musketry from the pursuing troopers came closer as his horse tired of the rapid pace. And, with the sure instinct of a born horseman, Jimmy Christopher flung himself from his mount to the side of the road, firing his revolver into the air as he did so. His horse, frightened by the shooting behind and startled by Jimmy Christopher's shot so close to his head, sprang ahead like a startled deer, while Jimmy rolled over and over on the ground, holding his elbows close to his sides to break the shock of the fall.

He had gauged his jump accurately, for he had noticed a tall rock jutting up from the landscape some twenty yards from the road.

The pursuing troopers, thinking that he had been shot from his horse, uttered mad shouts of victory and spurred gloatingly toward him. Jimmy Christopher came out of his roll with the litheness of a panther, and sprinted for the protection of the wide rock. He reached it just as a fusillade of shots burst out behind him. He threw himself headlong behind the rock, and the bullets from the Uhlans' carbines splintered the stone close to his head.

He thrust an arm over the rock, and emptied his revolver at

the troopers. He saw two of them drop from their mounts, saw the others rein in and break their charge. They had not expected their quarry to fight back in this way.

The troopers of the Purple Empire had been recruited by Emperor Rudolf from the cesspools of the world. Eurasians from Malaysia, half-breeds from the slums of Singapore, cringing peasants from Central Europe who had lived all their lives under the sway of a dictator, and others of like ilk made up the legions of the Purple Empire. These men fought well under the rigid discipline to which they were subjected. They could sweep over a countryside with ruthless savagery, or march irresistibly into an enemy town—after that countryside or that town had been subjected to a merciless barrage by their high-powered artillery. But in a hand-to-hand fight, where they were not supported by cannon, tanks, and airplanes, they could never hope to be a match for free American soldiers.

Thus, when Jimmy Christopher's first few shots struck down two of their number, they drew back a few paces, hesitating. And in that moment of respite Operator 5 reloaded his gun with fingers made swift by desperation. The troopers spread out in the road, and Jimmy could see that their purpose was to come at him from three sides at once. Against such an attack with high-velocity carbines, his revolver would be of little avail.

Grimly, he stood erect, disdaining further protection of the rock. He could not hope to fight them off for more than a few minutes, and it would be better to die this way. Streaks of fire flared from his revolver, as he fired slowly, accurately, picking off the nearest of the troopers. But the men were moving fast and accurate shooting in the night under these circumstances was difficult. He emptied his revolver with only two casualties among the enemy.

Now they were closing in on him. They knew his gun was empty. They were holding their fire. Perhaps they guessed that this man was no ordinary American spy. Perhaps they guessed that he was Operator 5 in person. That would mean a fabulous reward to the man who captured him. Jimmy Christopher pulled out a handful of cartridges from his pocket, flipped open the chamber of his gun, and began to reload desperately. He would never be able to make it. They would be upon him in a moment.

Now they had returned their carbines to the slings in their saddles and were drawing their long, cruelly sharp sabers. Their shouts filled the air as they rode down at him, sabers flashing in the night. Jimmy did not carry a sword. He had only his revolver, and he would not be able to get that loaded before the nearest horseman reached him.

It was at that moment that a shrill whistle pierced through the night with a raucous note of urgency. The blast of that whistle seemed to strike out at the charging troopers like an invisible beam of some potent electrical ray. Even as its echoes came back to them from the ridges to the north, the blast was followed by a single word shouted in a powerful, stentorian voice: *"Charge."*

And suddenly horses hooves drummed thunderously on the road as a compact body of men appeared out of the night, riding like an avenging army down upon the Uhlan patrol. Jimmy Christopher's face was transformed as he uttered a glad shout: "Tim! You little son-of-a-gun!"

For at the head of those charging men rode Tim Donovan, the freckle-faced boy who had escaped a few moments ago. The body of horsemen, Jimmy Christopher saw at a glance, was a contingent of MacPherson's Arizona Scouts. They wore the khaki blouses and the wide sombreros which MacPherson's Scouts had made famous throughout the occupied territory.

RIFLES CRACKED all about Jimmy Christopher, as MacPherson's men spread out riding down the Uhlans. The night was made hideous by the Purple troopers' shrieks of fear and cries for mercy. But no mercy was shown, no quarter given. The fight lasted less than five minutes and not a single Purple trooper was left alive. Tim Donovan came loping back to where Jimmy Christopher stood. The lad was panting as he leaped from his horse, and his lips quivered.

"Jimmy!" he exclaimed. "Are you all right? I—I was afraid we'd get here too late!"

Jimmy Christopher put both hands on the boy's shoulders, and pressed hard, affectionately.

"Good kid, Tim!" he said huskily. "I thought my number was up for a minute, before you came. Where did you meet MacPherson's men?"

"About a mile down the road. George MacPherson thought we might get in a jam, so he took fifty men and headed this way. I brought them back at the double-quick."

The Arizona Scouts were cantering over toward them now, having finished the job of mopping up. Young George MacPherson, their leader, dismounted, and shook Jimmy's hand eagerly.

"That was a close call, Operator 5! About a minute more, and we'd have been too late!"

Jimmy Christopher smiled. He had met young George many months before. George's father, Frank MacPherson, had once been the foremost chemist in America. He had volunteered with the American Defense Force in the early days of the Purple Invasion, and had lost an arm in the street fighting around Denver. His life had been spared by the Purple High Command, because his knowledge of chemistry was necessary to them.

Frank MacPherson now lived in Denver, under the rule of the invader, and he had secretly organized this troop of scouts. He had to spend some time in Denver, in order to lull the suspicions of the Governor of the Occupied Territory, and, during his frequent absences he left his son, George, in command.

"How's your father?" Jimmy Christopher asked.

George MacPherson frowned. "Dad's due to meet the troop tomorrow. But I'm worried about him. He takes too many risks, coming in and out of Denver. If the Purple patrols ever spot him, he's through. He'd quit Denver for good and come out to stay with the troop, if it wasn't for mother, and sis, and my kid brother, Jimmy. He could never get the whole family out of Denver."

Jimmy Christopher nodded. "I understand. But things are coming to a head fast. Tomorrow night at six is when we start the big push. After that, we'll either be free or dead. In the meantime, I've got to talk to your father tonight. We'll have to go into Denver."

The Arizona scouts had gathered about them, and were listening intently. George MacPherson looked dubious.

"I doubt if we could do it, Operator 5. The Purple High Command suspects there's something big in the wind, and they've trebled the guard around Denver. That's why I was worried about dad—"

"Well, we'll try it anyway," Jimmy told him. "I want about twenty of your men as volunteers, for a little special job that I've got in mind, after I see your father."

"A job?"

Jimmy's face was suddenly drawn, anxious. "You all know Diane Elliot, my fiancée?" *

---

* AUTHOR's NOTE: The name of Diane Elliot is well known to every reader of these chronicles who has followed the history of the Purple Invasion. This beautiful, talented girl, once the ace reporter for a great news syndicate, had been the first to defy the Purple Emperor when the mechanized troops of the enemy had invaded the United States. For that she had been sentenced to death, and had several times barely escaped from the cunning traps set by the Emperor and his shrewd Prime Minister, Baron Julian Flexner. Throughout the arduous days of the American defense against this war of aggression, she had linked her fortunes with those of Operator 5, and had followed him at the constant risk of her life. The ties between these two were far stronger than those of any ordinary lovers—for they denied themselves the consummation of their love in order to serve their country. But Jimmy Christopher, Diane Elliot and Tim Donovan would never hesitate to lay down their lives individually for the sake of one or the other of the three. We have just seen Jimmy Christopher do that for Tim Donovan.

They nodded. There was not one of them who had not heard of Diane Elliot. As Operator 5's trusted lieutenant, as well as his fiancée, she had often undertaken the most difficult and hazardous Intelligence assignments—assignments which many a man might have failed in. Her name was beloved throughout America. Some day, when the scars of the dreadful Purple Invasion have healed entirely, and America has been rebuilt from the smoldering ruins, men will have time to honor the heroes of that war—and Diane Elliot's name will assume its proper place among those to be honored for their sacrifice and bravery during those terrible times.

"Diane is working her way north from Colorado Springs," Jimmy Christopher told them swiftly. "She's been contacting our boys behind the enemy lines in that sector, and is to meet me with full reports in Denver today. I want about twenty men with me, in case we run into trouble."

George MacPherson grinned. "I don't think you'll have any trouble getting twenty volunteers, Operator 5. In fact, it'll be hard to keep the rest of the boys from going!"

"Let's start then," Jimmy Christopher said crisply. "We haven't got much time to lose!"

Two of the Uhlans' horses were recovered for the use of Jimmy and Tim, and the troop started out for Denver, riding cautiously through the night. George MacPherson threw out scouts ahead of them, to give warning if they should encounter other enemy patrols.

Young MacPherson, riding at Jimmy Christopher's right, said somberly: "The people in the Occupied Territory are all on edge, Operator 5. They're ready, waiting for you to say the word. Conditions have become intolerable."

"I know," Jimmy Christopher told him. "I've been behind the enemy lines a dozen times in the last couple of weeks—"

"It's worse than ever now," MacPherson broke in bitterly. "Tonight, the Purple High Command has gone the limit. They're entering every house in Denver, and taking out the eldest born. They're going to kill the first-born child of every family, if the American Defense Force starts its push tomorrow!"

Grimly, Operator 5 stared ahead into the night. "We'll try to stop that tonight!" he said tightly.

CHAPTER 3
THE ELDEST MUST DIE

THE ROOM was tense, utterly silent, except for the labored breathing of the four people who occupied it. Frank MacPherson with the stump of his right arm still swathed in bandages where it had been amputated above the elbow, puffed intently at his pipe. He was gripping the bowl of it in his left hand, not even feeling the heat which almost seared his palm. There was sweat on his forehead, and his great shock of iron-gray hair was uncombed.

Mrs. MacPherson sat on the edge of the easy chair, with an arm about her husband's shoulders. Young Jimmy MacPherson paced up and down restlessly, smoking cigarettes with furious intensity, while his sister, Nora, peered through the curtains out into the deserted streets of Denver.

From her vantage point Nora MacPherson could see across the old Municipal Golf Links to where a strange flag waved over the Colorado State Capitol Building. The streets were gray, almost white with the light of the growing dawn. From somewhere near by she could hear the ominous roll of a drum, and the tread of measured, marching feet. Her agitated breathing almost kept time with the beating of the drum.

She was pretty, dark-haired, perhaps four years the senior of young Jimmy MacPherson. Her white hand, gripping the curtain, tightened as the drum drew nearer. Suddenly, she uttered a gasp. Her eyes widened. A squad of soldiers turned the corner into their street. A drummer marched ahead of them, tapping out a sinister roll. That tune was no more sinister than the insignia painted in black upon the taut skin of the drum. It was the insignia of the Purple Empire, dreaded conquerors of America—the severed head and crossed broadswords.

Under that sign, Rudolph, Emperor of the Purple Empire, had marched across America with fire and sword. His flag, with the same symbol, flew even now over the Capitol Building. And his soldiers were marching through the streets of Denver at dawn, as they were marching through the streets of every other city in the Occupied Territory, upon a grim and bloody mission.

Nora MacPherson dropped the curtain, turned away from the window. The color that had come to her cheeks heightened her beauty, but the terror in her eyes made her a thing to pity rather than admire.

"T-they've come into our street!" she gasped.

Frank MacPherson tensed in his chair. "Take it easy, girl,"

he growled. "They'll be here in a moment. And you, Jimmy"—pointing the stem of his pipe at his son—"remember, keep your mouth shut, and don't give them any backtalk. We mustn't provoke them or arouse their suspicion—otherwise, they might search the house, and find the papers I've hidden. They'd execute everyone in the house—and, what's more, they'd have the name of every man in the ranks of MacPherson's Scouts!"

Mrs. MacPherson glanced up affectionately at her husband. "Aren't you taking a big chance, Frank—keeping those lists here?"

He shrugged. "Can't be helped, dear. Somebody has to take the chance. But if we talk softly to them, we'll get by." He fixed his deep-set eyes upon his youngest son. "Remember, Jimmy. You're a hot-tempered kid. So restrain yourself tonight, and no backtalk—"

Young Jimmy MacPherson's eyes blazed. He hurled his cigarette into the fireplace, and clenched his hands. "Damn it!" he shouted hoarsely. "How can you sit there so calmly, Dad? They've been going around all night, dragging people from their homes. If George were here, they'd take him, too, because he's the eldest." Jimmy took a step forward, shaking a finger in his father's face. "Do you hear? They'd take your eldest son. They'd take him with the hundreds and thousands of other eldest sons, and they'd crucify him. But you want me to control myself, not to give them any backtalk—"

He broke off as his father rose awkwardly from the easy-chair, pushing away his wife's offer of assistance. MacPherson towered above his young son.

"Jimmy," he said solemnly, "you wouldn't say that I was a coward, would you?"

Jimmy let his eyes rest for a fleeting moment upon the stump of his father's right arm. "N-no, dad."

"Then do as I say. There is no profit in defying these troopers. We must bide our time."

HE PUSHED past his son, went to the window and peered out. The monotonous beating of the drum was continuing with dreadful insistency. The troopers outside were going from house to house in this quiet residential street, and pounding upon the door until they were admitted. Already, a small group of young men prisoners were gathered in the street—young men who had been taken from the other houses.

And now, Frank MacPherson saw a burly sergeant cross toward his own door. In a moment, the sergeant was pounding at the door with the butt of his revolver.

MacPherson turned away from the window. He mumbled: "Stay here, everybody. I'll admit him."

He crossed the room, went out into the foyer. Mrs. MacPherson and her son and daughter waited, hardly breathing, while there came to them the sounds of the opening door, of the gruff voice of the sergeant, then of footsteps returning into the room. Frank MacPherson reentered, followed by the sergeant and two troopers with bayoneted rifles.

They seemed to fill the room, these Purple Empire troopers, clad in the drab gray of the conquering army, with their round-topped steel helmets, exuding the odor of unwashed beasts.

Nora MacPherson shrank back involuntarily from the beastliness of them, while young Jimmy faced them half-defiantly, fists clenched at his sides.

The sergeant wasted no time with preambles. He unrolled a scroll, glanced around the room, and proceeded to read—

"In accordance with a decree of our august master, Rudolph I, Emperor of the Purple Empire, Master of Europe and Asia, and Conqueror of America, you are hereby ordered to turn over into the custody of the Imperial Forces your eldest-born offspring to be held as a hostage. Whereas the American Defense Forces, under the leadership of one, Operator 5, have launched a counter-attack upon the Imperial Armies at the Continental Divide, it is decreed that if the said Operator 5 shall not withdraw his men from their trenches, the eldest born in each and every family within the Occupied Territory shall be executed!"

The sergeant ceased reading, and glanced around the room, his upper lip curling. "Well? Who is your eldest born?"

Frank MacPherson faced the trooper, standing erect, shoulders back, with the stump of his right arm hanging piteously at his side. "My eldest born is not here," he said quietly.

The sergeant grinned, consulted a long list which one of the troopers handed him. "You are Frank MacPherson. You lost your arm two months ago while defending a barricade here in the streets of Denver, against the Imperial troops. You were not executed because your services as an expert chemist were required."

Frank MacPherson bowed his head. "That is true. I have been

ordered to report to the chemical warfare factory for work start-
ing tomorrow—on pain of having my family executed."

The sergeant continued to read from the list. "You have one
son, George, twenty-six years old; a daughter, Nora, twenty-two,
and a son, James, nineteen. We want George MacPherson!"

"I already told you, Sergeant, he is not here."

The sergeant seemed to be enjoying himself, playing with the
old man, as a cat with a mouse. "We know where your eldest son
is, my friend. He has gone to volunteer with the army which
Operator 5 has gathered at the Continental Divide!"

Frank MacPherson's face was expressionless. "I know nothing
of that," he said tonelessly.

"That's right," the sergeant jeered. "None of you Americans
know about that volunteer army. It is strange how little you all
know when we question you. And you think that you are safe,
because your eldest born is not here, eh?"

Into Frank MacPherson's eyes there had come a momentary
nicker of uneasiness. "What do you mean?" he asked.

"Just this"—the sergeant's thick lips twisted in a sneer—"that
if your eldest born is not available, we will take the next oldest!"
He pushed across the room with three long, heavy strides, and
placed a thick-fingered hand upon the slender arm of Nora.

"This is your next oldest!" he said triumphantly. "We shall
take her. If your oldest son does not like the thought of his sister
as a hostage, let him come back from the American army, and
surrender himself!"

His grip tightened on Nora's arm. "Come, girl!"

NORA MacPHERSON'S face was suddenly as white as

the dawn outside. She seemed to congeal within herself, but she did not offer to resist as the sergeant half-dragged, half-led her across the room toward the door.

Frank MacPherson exclaimed: "No, no! You can't take women. And she's only a child—"

The sergeant laughed gruffly. "A child? She's old enough to be crucified with the rest!"

Young Jimmy was red in the face. "Wait, you beasts!" he shouted. "Wait. Take me instead. I'm a man. Take me—"

The Purple officer sneered. "Very noble of you, my boy." Suddenly, his tone changed from sneering tolerance to ugly brutishness. "Stand back. We're taking the girl!"

At a motion from him, the two troopers at the door leveled their bayonets at the stomach of young Jimmy, who had begun to rush forward. Jimmy caught himself up short in midstride, just in time to save himself from being impaled upon the two bayonets.

His father put his one good hand on the lad's shoulder. "Take it easy, Jimmy!" he whispered.

The boy restrained himself with a visible effort. There flashed through his mind stories of how whole households in the Occupied Territory had been bayoneted by the troopers of the Purple Empire, with the slightest provocation. He threw a quick side glance at his mother, who was standing behind the easy chair, trembling, her old, tortured eyes fixed in utter misery upon the slender daughter who was being dragged away.

Nora MacPherson did not attempt to resist. She forced

FRANK
MacPHERSON

NORA MacPHERSON

TIM DONOVAN

herself to smile wanly, and stammered: "Good-by. I—I'll be all right."

The sergeant marched her out of the room without another

word, and the two troopers swung
after him stiffly.

For two minutes there was not
a sound, not a movement in the
living-room, while they listened
intently to the receding steps of
Nora MacPherson and the three
soldiers.

At last, the front door slammed. Jimmy MacPherson breathed
a deep sigh. "Dad!" he exploded. "We can't let them do that to
Nora. My God—"

He stopped, the words dying on his lips at sight of the terrible
look in his father's face.

Frank MacPherson said slowly: "No, by God, we won't!
Jimmy, we've got to waylay that squad of troopers!"

"Waylay them? With what? We have no weapons." The boy
was frantic now.

The father's lips twisted in a grim smile. "Yes we have,
Jimmy. You didn't think MacPherson's Scouts fought with
their bare hands, did you? I didn't want you to know about the
guns—you're too hot-headed. Now—well, I guess I'm a little
hot-headed myself!"

He stepped to the fireplace, seized one of the andirons, and
pushed aside the smoldering logs, while his son and his wife
watched intently. Out in the street the measured tread of the
departing squad of Purple Empire troopers with their prisoners,
could be heard receding, to the accompaniment of the dismal
beating of the drum. But Jimmy and Mrs. MacPherson paid

no attention to that now, as they watched Frank MacPherson with his one hand, pulling at a rung set into the back wall of the fireplace.

A small section of brick came out, revealing a black opening. MacPherson reached into the opening and drew out a revolver, which he handed to Jimmy. Then he reached in again, brought out a short-barreled carbine, such as were carried by the carbineers of the Central Empire.

He laughed harshly. "I picked these up from dead Purple troopers in the street fighting here in the city. I hid them for the future. Now we'll use them!"

Jimmy was eagerly twirling the chamber of the revolver, to make sure that it was loaded. "We can cut across through the ruins in the next street," he said swiftly, "and ambush them. We could shoot them all down—"

Mrs. MacPherson put a hand on the stump of her husband's arm. "Frank! You were saving those guns for the signal, when Operator 5 is to attack. There are hundreds of other weapons hidden in other homes throughout the city. If it should be discovered that you had hidden guns, the Purple troops would search every house, and probably find them. That would ruin Operator 5's plan. Think now."

The one-armed man laughed bitterly. "Maybe so, Martha, but it can't be helped. If you think we're going to let Nora be taken away like this—"

He paused, smiled almost gently, stooped and kissed her. "We've got to do this, Martha. They're going to crucify all those prisoners. I'd sacrifice anything to save Nora from that!" He swung to his son. "Come on, Jimmy. We can just catch them!"

Mrs. MacPherson watched them leave. She stood in the same spot, in the middle of the room, never moving. There was a tear in the corners of her eyes, and her lips were trembling. She knew that the mad attempt which her husband and her son were about to make was almost hopeless. She did not expect to see either of them alive again. And she had to remain here, inactive, waiting—waiting, until she should hear news from them.

Slowly, she walked to the easy-chair, sank down into it, and sat there, immovable, staring into the grate, while tears from her wide-open eyes streaked her cheeks. In one moment of time she was seeing her daughter, her husband and her son snatched from her....

CHAPTER 4
THE SUN OF BLOOD

THERE WAS a time when Denver was the Queen City of Colorado. Its beautiful site, five thousand feet above sea level, had attracted countless visitors from the Middle West, and thousands of people had come here to live in the healthful, salubrious climate. Her tall white buildings, rising in friendly challenge to the imposing cliffs of the Continental Divide only fifteen miles away, had once been the pride and the glory of the Centennial State.*

Now those buildings were for the most part only a heap of ruins and charred debris. The heavy ordnance of the attacking Purple Army had leveled those buildings, destroyed the beautiful parks, wrecked streets, water-mains and electricity-generating plants. And throughout Colorado, in the sections where such intrepid explorers as De Soto, Escalante, Pike and Fremont had once trodden upon rich and virgin soil, the brutal servants of the Purple Emperor now walked arrogantly.

It was through these streets that the young prisoners, the first-born of Denver, were being led to the prison-camp.

Nora MacPherson, among the prisoners, was trying her best, to cheer up a young fellow of eighteen who walked beside her. She knew the chap by name. He was Terry Stone, who lived across the street from her. She had seen Terry taken from his house when she watched at the window, and she was sorry for

---

* AUTHOR's NOTE: It is interesting to note the history of the name and sobriquet of the State of Colorado. It was acquired by the United States in 1876, just one hundred years after the First War of Independence, and was therefore nicknamed, "The Centennial State." It was formerly inhabited by the Pueblo Cliff Dwellers, and was formed from territory included in the Louisiana Purchase, to which was added land acquired through the Texas and Mexican Cessions. The Mexican influence survives in the State's official name—Colorado being derived from the Spanish *colorar,* (to color) and which no doubt refers to the gorgeous natural coloration of the rocky formations to be found everywhere.

him. For, although he was only a year younger than her own brother Jimmy, there seemed to be a much greater difference in their ages. Terry Stone was only a boy yet, and he was taking this arrest pretty hard.

Looking at him sidewise, Nora could see his chin quivering, as he tried to control himself from bursting into tears. She put a hand on his arm.

"Chin up, Terry!" she said encouragingly. "We're not dead yet!"

Terry Stone turned his head toward her. "God, Miss MacPherson, they're g-going to crucify us. They'll nail us to wooden crosses. It—it hurts. God! Why do they have to be so cruel—"

A trooper marching near them poked the tip of his bayonet into the boy's back. "Silence!" he growled.

Terry Stone uttered an exclamation of pain as the sharp point of the bayonet gouged between his shoulder blades. The trooper laughed. "You will scream louder, little one, when Balku, the Executioner, begins to work on you!"

He spoke in the language of the Purple Empire, and fortunately neither Terry Stone nor the other young captives understood him. But Nora MacPherson, who had learned a good deal of the language, understood him only too well. And she shuddered, involuntarily.

Balku, the Imperial Executioner, was known and loathed throughout the Occupied Territory. His huge, gross, barrel-chested figure was familiar to American civilians everywhere. Of all the executioners in the empire, Rudolph the First had made Balku his favorite. Emperor Rudolph was himself a sadist, and he constantly sought for new methods of inflicting torture and death upon conquered peoples. Balku had provided himself with a heavy spiked ball, set on the end of an iron swagger-stick. With this spiked ball he would strike at the body and the face of a victim, until that victim was nothing but a mass of quivering, agonized flesh.

For that bit of fiendish ingenuity, Rudolph had made Balku his official executioner, and took him along wherever he traveled. No one knew the true nationality of the man, Balku, for no one had ever heard him speak. But the insensate brutality and sadistic fiendishness written upon his coarse countenance spoke more for the nature of the man than could any words that he might have uttered. And these young captives would be doubly unfortunate if they were to be delivered to the tender mercies of the Emperor's favorite executioner.

The mention of Balku by the trooper gave Nora MacPherson food for thought. If Balku was in Denver, it meant only one thing—that Emperor Rudolph was also here. At once her own plight was forgotten. That was important news. She must find some way to communicate it to her father. If Rudolph were in Denver, Operator 5 must be informed. Only a couple of days ago, Operator 5 had headed a raiding-party through the lines, in a mad effort to capture the Emperor. There had been a fight, and Rudolph had been seen to sway upon his horse as if wounded. Whether he had been hit or not, Operator 5 did not know, for the Emperor had escaped from the trap.* That attempt had failed, but another attempt might succeed. Nora decided that she must get the news of Rudolph's presence in Denver to Operator 5 at any cost.

THEY WERE marching now through the southeast section of the city, where the damage had been greatest. Nora could see across a dozen square blocks, over miles of debris. Not a building had been left standing in this part of town. Even the streets were rutted and torn where huge high-explosive shells had fallen. Ahead of them, perhaps a half-mile away, she could see the stockade of the concentration camp where they were being taken. In there she knew she would find hundreds of other American civilians, both men and women, living under almost impossible conditions, exposed to the inclemencies of the weather, subsisting on the most miserable of rations.

And at the same time she knew that dozens of other Purple patrols were escorting other groups of young people to that same concentration camp—the first step toward a horrid death at the hands of Balku, the Executioner.

Livid tinges of dawn were empurpling the eastern sky, and

---

* Author's Note: Reference is here made to the incident related in the last issue of this periodical, in the story entitled, "Drums of Destruction." The feud between Emperor Rudolph and Operator 5 had become more or less a personal one, as we have seen from the preceding pages. That enmity was more invidious on the Emperor's side than it was on that of Jimmy Christopher. Operator 5 was interested mainly in eliminating a sinister enemy of America, while Rudolph hated him as a man.

great gobs of color shown upon the ridges of the Continental Divide to the west. There, she thought bitterly, were the thousands of American patriots, waiting for zero hour and the big push. What would they do when they learned that the first-born of their families—their own children whom they loved and for whom they were fighting—would be atrociously murdered when the big push started? Would they go over the top? Would they attack, knowing that the attack would cost them the lives of their own children?

The devilish ingenuity of the Purple High Command in ordering this round-up of youngsters was brought home to her with brutal force. This was a *coup* of which only Rudolph was capable—Rudolph, perhaps the most debauched, debased man ever to have acquired supreme power in the history of the world.

And that man was here in Denver now, where a bold stroke on the part of Operator 5 might reach him. The more she thought of it, the more important it began to seem to her to get this information to Operator 5; for she realized fully that the only way to prevent the slaughter of these innocents—it was characteristic of her that she did not consider her own fate—was to get at Rudolph in some way.

Desperately, she cast about her for some means of escape. But it looked hopeless. The burly sergeant who had dragged her out of her home marched at the head of the patrol. Three troopers with bayoneted guns marched on either side of the line of captives, while four or five others brought up the rear. And she knew only too well that these troopers would not hesitate to shoot to kill at the first sign of an attempt at escape.

They were crossing Cherry Creek now, moving in the direction of the old Polo Grounds, where the concentration camp had been set up. The bridge across the creek had been destroyed in the bombardment of Denver, and  a crude structure had been erected for temporary use. Nora MacPherson glanced furtively behind her. This was as good a chance as she would ever have to escape. A leap from this bridge, a quick run, and she could take refuge in the crumbling masonry of a wrecked building off the road.

They might get her with rifle-fire before she could reach the protection of the ruins, but that was a chance she would have to take. She threw a quick glance at the guard marching beside her. The man was looking ahead, holding his carbine ready. She could dodge behind him and slip over the railing before his sluggish wits could grasp the significance of what she was attempting.

She tensed, and her muscles tautened. A strange, quivering coldness pervaded her body. She had never been called upon before to face the menace of deadly carbines spouting lead. Within the next two minutes she might be dead, a pitiful, twisted heap of still warm flesh at the side of the road. And she wanted so much to live. She was young yet; she could get so much from life. If the Purple troops were driven out of America, life could become peaceful and happy once more. But if she sacrificed herself now, she would not be alive to enjoy that peace and that happiness.

40

Resolutely, she thrust those thoughts from her. She steeled herself for the ordeal.

SHE GLANCED at the nearest trooper, saw that she was unobserved; and began to edge toward the right, toward the railing of the bridge. And at that instant she heard a sound that wrenched at her already taut nerves; a sound that sent a chill of excitation through her system, and kept her in line with the other captives. That sound was innocent enough in itself—it was the short, sharp, whimpering bark of a distant prairie dog.

Prairie dogs were numerous in Denver now. Since the city had been laid in ruins, the small animals had come into town in droves, and their little mound-like burrows could be seen everywhere. Often the night was made hideous by their barking calls. But this particular bark was just different enough from the usual sound to have a significance of its own for Nora MacPherson while it was natural enough to avoid attracting the attention of the Purple troopers.

It was the call which Nora knew her father's troop of scouts to use when they wished to signal to one another. To distinguish it from the authentic whine of the real prairie dogs, they generally appended a little trill at the end, which could never fool a true Westerner, but which the untrained ears of the invading troopers failed to catch entirely.

And that call which Nora had just heard was surely the call of MacPherson's Scouts—unless the taut condition of her nerves had fooled her ears. Tensely, she glanced around, seeking some confirmation of the sound she had heard. They were crossing the bridge quickly now, and her chance to escape would be gone in a moment.

The trooper alongside her glanced her way, saw that the girl was quivering with excitement, and put it down to fear. He laughed harshly, and pushed her with a rough hand, so that she stumbled sideways into young Terry Stone.

"Back in line, girl!" he growled. "Or you get a bayonet through your stomach!"

Nora stumbled ahead, with Terry Stone supporting her. "Buck up, Miss MacPherson," he said. "Remember what you told me before."

Nora nodded wordlessly, and forced a smile. They were coming off the bridge now. It was too late to make her bid for freedom. Tears glistened in her eyes. The bark of that prairie dog had fooled her. She had been overwrought, and had mistaken it for the call of the scouts.

Or had it really been a signal? Suddenly, she stiffened. There it was again, coming from somewhere on the right! Distinctly, she heard that little trill at the end. And again, from the left, the call was repeated. MacPherson's Scouts were here. She was sure of it now!

Eagerly, her eyes searched the debris on either side of the column, for some sign of them. She could see nothing.

And then abruptly her ears caught the creak of wagon wheels behind them.

The sergeant in command of the patrol heard that wagon, too, and he turned around. Nora and the young prisoners gazed behind them also, and saw that an old, wobbling wagon was coming up on the bridge that they had just crossed, and heading along the street to pass them.

Beside the wagon rode a swaggering young captain of Intelligence of the Imperial Army. The wagon was being driven by a man, and a freckle-faced boy sat beside the driver. Two horses were hitched to that wagon, and had the Purple sergeant been at all observing it would have seemed strange to him that two such fine animals should be used for such a lowly purpose.

Looking through the open front of the wagon behind the driver, Nora could see that there were bulky objects within it, covered by large tarpaulins.

But she had no time for any of that. Her eyes merely flickered over the horses, rested in eager wonder upon the driver. For the driver of that wagon was her own brother, George MacPherson!

She half raised her arm, and a glad cry bubbled to her lips, only to be repressed as she suddenly realized what she had been about to do. She glanced about fearfully, lest her involuntary action had been seen. But the troopers were not looking at her. **THE SERGEANT** grunted an order, and the column resumed its march. The sergeant did not even think to stop and question that wagon, for it was apparently convoyed by an Intelligence officer. George MacPherson was dressed in civilian clothes now, and the freckle-faced boy beside him might be a younger brother. It was quite common in the Occupied Territory for civilians to be impressed into service by officers. And since the failure of the gasoline supplies in the United States, horse-drawn vehicles were used almost exclusively—except where civilians were forced to pull them.

Nora MacPherson fell into step alongside Terry Stone, and her shoulders went back as a surge of joy rushed through her. Then it was true! Her ears had not deceived her. MacPherson's Scouts *were* here. Those prairie-dog calls had really been signals. They were going to rescue them!

And abruptly her spirits fell. She realized how impossible it would be for any group of men to effect a rescue here, in the heart of Denver, with enemy troops everywhere. It was a foolish, impossible undertaking. George must not attempt it. He would be killed.

She began to feel cold chills of apprehension as the column neared the concentration camp. Now they were within a half block of it, and the wagon was still behind them, proceeding slowly. Nora could see the barbed-wire fence of the camp, with the faces of the prisoners peering out at them. A guard tower near the gate was manned by a guard with a rifle, and other guards patrolled outside along the length of the barbed-wire fence. Once inside that stockade, there would be little chance to escape. And Nora knew that her brother would try to rescue her before she entered.

How he had found her, how he had learned that she was a prisoner, she could not guess. She knew that George was away with the scouts. Seeing him here in the city was a shock to her. And she could not understand who the Purple Intelligence officer might be who was riding beside the wagon. He had seemed very young and very haughty. Perhaps he was one of the scouts disguised as an enemy officer. But what could they do against the numerous guards around the stockade of the concentration camp? That there were other scouts in the immediate neighborhood, she was sure.

Her gaze strayed desperately in every direction, and she spotted a half dozen men leading a group of horses, some fifty yards away. They, too, were dressed in civilian garb, and the horses were saddled, fully equipped. They likewise attracted no attention on the part of the sergeant or the troopers of the patrol, who, if they gave any thought at all to the matter, assumed that the horses were remounts for the Imperial Cavalry, requisitioned by the Purple Quartermaster's Corps.

But Nora MacPherson, keyed up to a high pitch of tension, recognized those men as members of her father's scouts. She began to breath rapidly. Something was going to happen any minute now!

CHAPTER 5
THE LIGHTNING STRIKES

A S NORA MacPHERSON and her fellow prisoners approached the gate of the concentration camp in company with her fellow captives, the Purple troopers failed to notice the sudden air of tension that had suddenly spread over the district. They were now within a hundred feet of the gate, and they had no reason to fear an attack, in the heart of the city, with hundreds of troops in the vicinity. To them, the possibility of a hopeless and desperate attempt by desperate men, to rescue those they loved, was beyond comprehension.

But had they known the true identity of the driver of that

wagon, or of the pseudo-captain of Intelligence who rode along-side it, they might not have been so confident. In fact, if they could have overheard the conversation between the captain and the driver at that very moment, they would have believed both of them to be mad.

George MacPherson was reining in the horses, so as to keep the wagon from approaching the gate too quickly. Tim Dono-van, beside him, was fingering the butt of the revolver snugly hidden in his waistband. Jimmy Christopher, riding his mount with all the affected arrogance of a Purple officer, reined over close to the wagon and spoke out of the side of his mouth, keep-ing his eyes on the troopers ahead.

"Hold it back, George," he ordered. "We've got to give them time to open the gate."

George MacPherson nodded. "There are the other boys, coming up from the east, with the horses. Everything is work-ing on schedule. If the plan clicks—"

"It *has* to click!" Jimmy Christopher said tightly. "We can't afford to fail!" He threw a quick side-glance at the rear of the wagon where the tarpaulin-covered objects had begun to shift about slightly.

"Hold still, you men!" he snapped. "Don't move that tarpaulin. Be ready when I give the signal!"

Under that tarpaulin were hidden ten of MacPherson's men, together with Frank MacPherson and Jimmy. The balance of the contingent, that had accompanied Operator 5 into Denver, were distributed in the neighborhood, some with the horses that were being led toward the gate of the camp, others strolling apparently aimlessly in the neighborhood.

Almost all of those men had one or more relatives or friends in that concentration camp. They knew what it meant to be an inmate of one of the Imperial concentration camps. And now that they had the opportunity, there was no doubt as to how they would act when the moment came to fight.

Jimmy Christopher, slowing up his mount to accommodate himself to the pace of the wagon, surveyed the scene swiftly. Two machine-gun emplacements were located outside the camp, some fifty feet from the gate, and were manned by two troopers each. They were placed there, not to repel an attack from outside, but to prevent a concerted rush of prisoners from within. Both machine guns were trained on the gate.

A small barracks building had been erected off to the right of the gate, and here, Jimmy Christopher knew from information given him by MacPherson, there were some fifty or sixty troopers, permanently assigned to concentration-camp duty. Those in the barracks would be off duty now, and most probably asleep. A corporal and six guards were stationed at the guardhouse alongside the gate, and sentries patrolled the entire circumference of the barbed-wire at fifty-foot intervals. The camp, itself, Jimmy had learned, covered some five acres of ground, and contained some eight hundred prisoners at this time.

Those prisoners were compelled to sleep in the open, with no protection from rain or cold except for the few miserable blankets that their relatives and friends sent them.

And Jimmy could see that most of those prisoners had assem-

The youngsters ran into the mêlée,
using their guns as clubs.

bled just inside the fence to witness the arrival of the new prisoners. But they kept a good distance from the gate, doubtless due to orders from their guards. That was how Jimmy wanted it.

As for the odds, he disregarded them. He had only twenty-three men, counting Tim Donovan. Those twenty-three must
carry out a surprise attack against some seventy or eighty troop-

ers, not counting the sentries stationed around the barbed-wire enclosure—and not counting the possible reinforcements that could be rushed here from other parts of the city once the alarm spread.

The chances of success were very slim. But he had given his promise, and he meant to go through with it.

HE HAD ridden in, a little while ago, with George MacPherson and the scouts. In the streets of Denver they had spotted this patrol marching toward the concentration camp, and they had also met old Frank MacPherson and his young son, Jimmy, stalking the patrol, planning to attack it to save Nora.

Frank MacPherson was seeing red, and insisted on attacking at once. Jimmy Christopher, with a deeper plan in mind, persuaded the old man to listen to him.

"Can you get weapons?" he asked.

"Yes. But—"

"And can you get a covered wagon, one that'll hold plenty of guns and some men?"

"Yes. We have guns—"

"All right. There's no time to waste. This patrol will make other stops. They won't reach the concentration camp for over an hour. Get the weapons, get the wagon, and meet us near the camp. We'll do more than rescue Nora, Mac—we'll strike a blow at the Purple Empire that they won't forget for a long time!"

And so it was that Operator 5 was riding beside the wagon, while MacPherson's men skulked in the debris about the concentration camp.

Now, the wagon had come almost to a complete stop, as the

sergeant and his detail paused before the gate. The corporal in charge of the sentries saluted, grinning wickedly at the pitiful, bedraggled-looking prisoners. He raised his eyebrows at sight of Nora MacPherson, who was the only girl in the group of captives, although there were a number of women among those already in the concentration camp.

The corporal turned and threw an order at one of the guards, who relayed it to another guard inside the barbed-wire fence. Almost at once the tall gate began to swing open, and the troopers started to herd their prisoners inside.

This was the moment for which Jimmy Christopher had been waiting. The gate was swung wide open now, and the prisoners were moving through. The two machine guns were trained upon the opening, and the entire attention of the troopers was concentrated upon them.

Jimmy Christopher drew a whistle from his pocket, and threw a final glance around to make sure that everything was set. He saw Tim Donovan watching him intently, tautly; and he smiled encouragingly at the lad. George MacPherson, tightly gripping the reins of his horses, had been watching the prisoners with anguished eyes, following his sister's slim figure as she was pushed through the gate with the others. He tore his gaze from Nora's back and looked at Jimmy.

"Now!" he said hoarsely. "For God's sake, Operator 5, give the signal!"

Jimmy nodded. He put the whistle to his lips, and blew two sharp, shrill blasts.

At once, the whole scene was transformed into one of swift,

sure action. The men who had been leading the horses stopped stock still, while a dozen of MacPherson's Scouts who had been hiding behind a pile of debris leaped out and raced toward them. These men vaulted into the saddles without a single lost motion, and spurred toward the Purple troopers at the gate, firing their rifles as they rode.

Jimmy Christopher shouted to George MacPherson, "Go ahead, George! You know what to do!" And he raced away from the wagon to meet the charging scouts and assume command of them.

IN THE meantime, George MacPherson wheeled the wagon around. The tarpaulin in the rear was violently thrown aside, revealing old one-armed Frank MacPherson, his younger son, Jimmy, and five more of the scouts. Beside them in the wagon, where it had also been hidden by the tarpaulin, lay a stack of rifles and hand grenades. The time had come for action.

Frank MacPherson barked orders, and his men seized grenades, leaped from the wagon, and ran toward the gate. Tim Donovan and George MacPherson, on the driver's seat, both picked up rifles from the floorboard, and, kneeling in front of the seat, they began to fire methodically at the guards around the gate.

The Purple troopers, taken by surprise, turned to run. Three or four of them fell under the fire of the scouts. A captain came running from the barracks building, and shouted at them wildly. They broke their mad flight, and swung their mounts around to meet the charge.

Jimmy Christopher had swung in ahead of the scouts, and he

was the first to clash with the enemy. If the troopers thought it queer that a Purple Empire Intelligence officer should be leading a raid upon them, they had no time to ruminate upon the question. For Jimmy's sword was swirling in the air, and he cut down the nearest trooper. The man fell from his horse, and at once a half dozen other troopers were around Operator 5 like a swarm of hornets, thrusting at him with their bayoneted rifles.

The scouts behind Jimmy rode into the thick of the mêlée, and in a moment the air became thick with swirling dust, burnt gunpowder, the shouts of fighting men and the shrieks of the wounded.

The scouts were outnumbered by at least three to one, and the troopers saw at a glance that this was only a handful of desperate men who were attacking them. The captain who had come from the barracks building rallied, calling to them in the language of the Purple Empire.

"They are only a handful!" he shouted. "Kill them!"

Jimmy Christopher and the half dozen scouts were virtually surrounded now, fighting grimly, silently.

Jimmy parried the thrust of a bayonet, ran his sword through the throat of the trooper, and threw a hurried glance about to see if MacPherson's end of the plan was being carried out. He had no time for more than a fleeting glimpse, for the troopers were thick around him. But he saw enough to satisfy him. Two of the men from the wagon were racing toward the barracks building, with grenades. Another had already reached the guardhouse at the gate of the concentration camp, and was in the act of hurling a grenade at it when Jimmy saw him.

The grenade, accurately hurled, went through the window of the guardhouse and exploded instantaneously, causing the mortar round the window to crumble.

Almost at the same moment the two men at the barracks building hurled their grenades. The black spheres fell just within the open doorway, and detonated with thunderous violence. The whole front of the barracks building collapsed, effectively blocking the doorway, so that the troopers inside would not be able to come to the relief of their fellows in the square.

THE GUARDS within the concentration camp had begun hastily to swing the gate shut at the first sign of attack. But the explosion of the guardhouse had wrecked the gate. Now, two of the men from the wagon ran though the entrance, shouting to the prisoners.

"Everybody out!" they called. "Go to the wagon! There are rifles for all of you. If you want your freedom, fight for it!"

A wild shout of glee went up from the prisoners, and they began to stream out through the gate, literally swamping the guards. They ran madly past the battled cavalrymen in front of the gate, heading for the wagon. There were fully three hundred of them, and as they reached the wagon, Tim Donovan, who had climbed into the rear, handed them rifles and ammunition, as well as grenades.

"Get in there and clean them up, boys!" Tim Donovan shouted. "That's Operator 5, in the Purple captain's clothes. Take orders from him!"

The prisoners, most of them under nineteen, had been for a long time subjected to the indignities and cruelties of the

Purple troopers. They welcomed this opportunity to repay them.

The youngsters ran into the mêlée, many of them using their guns as clubs to strike at the mounted troopers fighting the scouts. In a moment the tables were turned, the odds reversed. Instead of being outnumbered, the Americans now outnumbered the troopers.

The Purple soldiers, seeing themselves attacked by hundreds of the youths whom they had treated harshly as prisoners, gave way to sudden fear. One of them reined his horse sharply out of the fight, and spurred away past the barracks house. Another and another followed him.

Almost at once the square was cleared of Purple troopers, except for those still confined within the barracks building. Some of these had been sniping at the Americans from the upstairs windows. But now, Jimmy Christopher, taking command of the undisciplined prisoners, rapped out a string of orders. The youngsters, at his direction, scattered around the square, taking cover wherever possible, and opened up a withering fire at all the windows of the barracks buildings. The rolling crackle of three hundred rifles filled the air, beating against the walls of the barracks, and waking up the whole city of Denver. Almost immediately, the sniping ceased.

Five of the scouts ran forward under cover of the barrage, and hurled grenades into the upper windows of the barracks.

Thunderous explosions sounded within, and black smoke

curled out from the windows as well as from the wide, yawning cracks in the masonry which had been caused by the grenades.

Jimmy Christopher, watching from his position at the gate of the camp, smiled grimly as he saw a hand thrust out from one of the windows, waving a white flag. The soldiers in the barracks building were surrendering!

Frank MacPherson, who had seized the mount of a slain Purple trooper, came galloping over to him, managing the horse with his one hand. He was grinning broadly, elated at the victory.

"It's a clean-up, Operator 5!" he exclaimed. "By God, we'll take the city!"

Jimmy shook his head soberly. "I doubt it, MacPherson. There are about ten thousand enemy troops in Denver. Take command of these people. Get possession of the barracks. We'll want all the rifles and ammunition we can find in there."

MacPherson nodded, and rode off, shouting orders. He rounded up a dozen of his scouts, whom he appointed to act as junior officers. These men hastily divided the freed prisoners into platoons and companies, and a small detachment of them marched into the barracks to accept the surrender of the Purple soldiers.

JIMMY CHRISTOPHER'S mind was racing. This raid on the concentration camp was turning out to be more successful than he had dared to hope. He now had three hundred men under his command. And his problem was how best to employ them. He knew that he would have to get out of Denver as fast as possible. Because, despite MacPherson's enthusiastic desire to capture the city, the wisest move would be a retreat. Three hundred undisciplined youths could not hope to combat a whole division of Purple troops.

He watched MacPherson skillfully whipping his new recruits into shape, while the Purple soldiers were being marched out of the barracks. MacPherson kept sending in groups of the youths, and they came out carrying cases of rifles and ammunition which had been stored in the cellar. They loaded as much as they could onto the wagon, while other men went in search of more vehicles.

Groups of American civilians were gathering here in the square, attracted to the neighborhood by the shooting. They were all men. Their women were remaining within the protection of their homes. These men, seeing what had happened, began to talk agitatedly among themselves. Several of them looked queerly at Jimmy Christopher, who was still attired in his Purple captain's uniform.

Jimmy had not given it a thought, but now, seeing their glances, he smiled. He spurred his horse over toward the wagon, where the men were loading the cases of ammunition. From under the driver's seat he removed an American Army officer's tunic. He took off the Purple uniform, and donned the American tunic.

As he was buttoning it up, Tim Donovan came toward him, with Nora and George MacPherson. The three of them had been talking excitedly together near the shattered gate of the concentration camp. George MacPherson said eagerly, "Operator 5, you know my sister, Nora? She wants to thank you—"

Jimmy interrupted swiftly, "Never mind the thanks, Miss

MacPherson. It was something we had to do, and it's your father's scouts who made it possible." He swung on George. "Tell your father to muster the men. I see they've found two more wagons for the guns and ammunition. We'll have to pull out of here fast. Do you hear the bugles at the other end of the city? They're just getting the reports of what's happened. We'll have the whole garrison of Denver down on us, if we wait much longer—"

Nora MacPherson took an impulsive step forward. "Operator 5!" she exclaimed. "I've something important to tell you. I learned it from one of the troopers!"

Jimmy saw that the girl was deeply agitated. "Yes?" he asked.

Nora said slowly, "The trooper told me that Balku, the Executioner, was going to torture the prisoners. You know what that means?"

Frank MacPherson had come up to the group, just in time to hear what his daughter said. He stared at her blankly.

"Balku?" he repeated. "What of him? Suppose he *was* going to work on the prisoners? He won't get the chance now—"

Nora waved her father to silence. "It's not that, Dad." Her eyes were on Jimmy Christopher. "You see—"

Jimmy nodded. "Yes," he said slowly. "I see. If Balku, the Executioner, is here, *it means that Rudolph is in Denver!*"

Frank MacPherson snapped his fingers. "Of course! Why didn't I think of that! If the Emperor is here, we better get out fast—"

"On the contrary!" Jimmy said softly. "If Rudolph is in Denver, *then we stay!*"

Tim Donovan uttered a shout of glee. "Yeah! Then we're really going to try to take the town?"

"Right, Tim!" Jimmy Christopher swung on MacPherson. "What do you say? We've got three hundred armed men. We can arm five hundred more civilians with the stores we've just taken from the barracks. Shall we make a try to capture Rudolph with eight hundred men—against ten thousand? It's desperate, mad, hopeless. But it's a chance!"

Frank MacPherson's eyes were shining. With his good hand he was caressing the stump of his amputated arm. "I'm with you, Operator 5—to the limit!"

He extended his hand, and the two men shook with a firm grip.

"To the limit!" Jimmy Christopher repeated after him.

ABRUPTLY, OPERATOR 5 became the brisk, crisp commander which he could be in an emergency. "Muster your men, Mac!" he ordered. "Have them rip up cobblestones and paving-blocks, and round up timber for barricades. We'll barricade the streets. There'll be Purple troops here in a few minutes."

He swung on the others in the group. "George, get hold of five of your father's scouts. I want them to get out of Denver as quickly as possible, and spread the word among the local leaders in the neighborhood that a revolt has started in the city. Every American civilian within a radius of fifty miles, who has a weapon of any kind, is to march to Denver. I want every road blocked, with riflemen and snipers to command every pass, so that Rudolph can't escape, and so that fresh reinforcements for the Purple garrison won't be able to get through. Is that clear?"

George MacPherson nodded, eager-eyed. "I understand, Operator 5. I know just where to send the boys. I'll need about ten rather than five."

"Take them. And after you've given them their instructions, I want you, yourself, to do something else. You're to work your way across town to the old Curtis Aviation Field. About five hundred feet west of the field, there's an old farmhouse, in ruins. Across the road from the farmhouse is an old, dilapidated barn. That's where Miss Diane Elliot is to meet me. She has a dozen carrier-pigeons, ready to go with the signal for revolt to local leaders throughout Colorado, Wyoming and New Mexico. You are to tell Miss Elliot to release pigeons for all the Colorado and Wyoming leaders, with orders to march on Denver at once, without waiting for the zero hour. Understand?"

George MacPherson saluted briskly. He swiftly repeated the instructions to make sure he had them right, then hurried off.

"You, Miss MacPherson, and you, Tim," Jimmy went on quickly, "go talk to those civilians." He waved his hand toward the small groups who had formed everywhere in the square, and who were watching the preparations. "Tell them we're ready to strike. Any of them who are willing to fight, can have guns and ammunition. Let them fall in with the other men." He smiled grimly. "You shouldn't have any trouble in enlisting them, a hundred percent!"

Tim Donovan and Nora MacPherson hurried off to talk to the civilians.

Jimmy Christopher turned to survey the scene about him. The young men who had just been prisoners of the Purple Empire

JIMMY CHRISTOPHER

were now working everywhere, loading the wagons, tearing up paving-blocks and searching the debris for suitable material for barricades. Others were moving to form a wide circle about the square, so as to meet the attack of the Purple garrison when it came.

Jimmy Christopher called to a small group of men who seemed to have nothing to do. "Get those machine guns," he ordered, indicating the two weapons that were mounted to command the gate of the concentration camp. "Move them inside the barbed wire, and set them up so they can rake the square."

The men nodded, and went to work with a will.

Frank MacPherson came up to Jimmy, wiping sweat from his forehead with his one good hand. "I've got things moving, Operator 5," he said cheerfully. "God, it's good to be striking a blow for America again, after all these months of inactivity! Even if we fail, and die for our pains, I won't regret it!"

"We can't afford to fail, Mac!" Jimmy told him grimly. "Now, here's my plan."

He took a piece of chalk from his pocket, bent and began to draw a rough diagram on the cement road. "Now, here's the concentration camp. I'm having those machine guns moved into it, so that we can have a base to retreat to in case we're hard-pressed. We could hold this spot, behind the barbed-wire, for hours, till the Americans from the countryside arrive. But that's only in case of emergency."

MacPherson nodded. "Okay, Operator 5. But what do we do first?"

"We march on the State Capitol Building. That's where Rudolph would be, if he's in Denver. We should have our full eight hundred men within an hour, because word will be spreading through town fast. Now we'll send three hundred men up along Cherry Creek, to attack from the west. Three hundred more will march up York Street, through Cheesman Park, and attack from the east. The remaining two hundred men will stay here, as reserve."

He raised his head, as the ominous thrumming of drums sounded far off to the north. "The Purple troops are mustering to attack. Perhaps they don't know yet, in just what part of town the disturbance is. But they'll get word pretty soon. I'm counting on some of the Imperial Guards being sent away from the State Building. That'll help. Now as the Americans from the countryside begin to arrive, the enemy will have to throw more and more troops into the outlying districts to fight them off. That will help us."

"Sounds good to me," said Frank MacPherson. "When do we start?"

"Right now!" Jimmy Christopher said. "You'll take charge of the attacking party along Cherry Creek, and I'll take the one along York Avenue—"

"Nothing doing!" MacPherson rapped. "One of my scouts will take the York Avenue party. You're staying right here, in command. We've got to have somebody here to give orders to the civilians coming into town, and to direct the whole thing. Sorry, Operator 5, but you'll have to miss the fun this time!"

"All right," Jimmy Christopher admitted grudgingly. "Go to it, Mac. And good luck to you!"

His eyes were shining with fierce, patriotic fire as he thought how very soon now might come the hour when glorious liberty was at hand.

CHAPTER 6
EMPEROR OF EVIL

S UCH WAS the inception of the Great Denver Raid.* At the first break of dawn, Denver had been just another city in the Occupied Territory, overhung with the pall of fear and

---

* AUTHOR'S NOTE: The story of the Great Denver Raid is, of course, well known to all of us in its larger aspects. It has assumed its place in the history of our nation beside those other milestones such as Bunker Hill and the Boston Tea Party. Once the raid was begun, so many things were happening in so many parts of the city, that it is difficult to relate them all chronologically, or in the order of their importance. Therefore, if any reader finds that an important portion of the action has seemingly been slighted, it is not due to the fact that the author has overlooked it, but that he has been compelled to omit it for the sake of relating some of the incidents which bear upon our own characters. Many of those incidents have not been touched upon in standard textbooks as the information concerning them has not been available to historians. For instance, the hand-to-hand fight with Balku, the Executioner, was never made public until revealed in the private memoirs of Operator 5. Also various versions have been advanced as to Operator 5's motive in planning the raid. Many historians have believed it to have been long premeditated by Operator 5. As a matter of fact, the true version of the inception of the raid has been for the first time related in the preceding chapter. Jimmy Christopher never planned that raid until Nora MacPherson informed him that Rudolph I was in Denver. This explains why he was compelled to use the callow youths from the concentration camp; and it may also explain many of the queer incidents which follow.

repression, rendered somber by the iron rule of the conquering Purple Empire.

But an hour after dawn, Denver was a different city. Turmoil and confusion filled her streets. Purple troopers were massing everywhere, secure in their might, confident that within a few hours they would stamp out this daring rebellion. Due to the fact that two brigades of infantry were quartered in the city on their way to the front lines, the Purple troops in Denver numbered slightly over ten thousand.

As it was, there was little doubt in the Imperial Headquarters as to the outcome. In fact, so great was Emperor Rudolph's confidence, that he did not even bother to send for additional troops from outside the city.

He had established his headquarters in the State Capitol, and when the first news of the raid was brought to him he was in the vaulted basement of the building, amusing himself by watching his favorite executioner, Balku.

The basement had been converted into a huge dungeon and torture chamber, and it was here that Rudolph spent a good deal of his time, satisfying his sadistic thirst for the sight of human pain and suffering.

There were perhaps fifty chosen prisoners here. One of them, a tall, mustached man of about forty, was chained to a cross-beam in the shape of a cross, which was erected in the center of the room. He was stripped to the waist, and sweat was glistening from his forehead, trickling down his cheeks.

Opposite the torture cross, Emperor Rudolph I was seated

in a high-backed easy-chair, watching the expression on the prisoner's face.

Rudolph was smiling twistedly, cruelly. "Joseph Randall," he said in that coldly drawling voice of his, which had come to be hated throughout America, "you have five minutes in which to talk. After that, my friend Balku will have a free hand with you."

Rudolph indicated with a nod the figure of Balku, the Executioner, who stood a little to the left of the Emperor. Balku was a huge man, barrel-chested, with a queerly shaped, hydrocephalus head. The man was entirely bald, and his heavy chin seemed to be resting upon the thick, animal-like neck. His eyes were set closely together, and were mere slits. He wore only a pair of trousers and a short, waistcoat-like jacket, which revealed the muscles rippling across his immense torso, indicating a huge store of brute strength. In his right hand he gripped a three-foot rod made of heavy wood, perhaps three-quarters of an inch in diameter. At one end of this rod was attached an iron, spiked ball about the size of a grapefruit. The spikes were discolored with clotted blood, as was also Balku's jacket and hairy chest. He was looking at Joseph Randall, with a leering smile upon his twisted lips.

"It would be better, master," he said to Rudolph, speaking in a jargon of mixed European dialects which was extremely difficult to understand, "if you would let me give him to the jaguar. My jaguar is very hungry, and he will tear this man apart beautifully. What do you say?"

Rudolph frowned. "No, Balku. That jaguar shall not eat until I can feed him with the body of Operator 5, or of Operator 5's woman—that Elliot girl!" He raised a white, pudgy hand, and pointed a finger at the prisoner tied to the cross. "Well, Randall, will you talk? You have only to tell me what I want to know, and you will be spared the tender mercies of Balku."

Randall remained silent, his level eyes meeting those of Rudolph, defiantly.

The Emperor went on impatiently: "You are one of the leaders of the guerrilla troops of the Americans who have been forming in the Occupied Territory under the direction of Operator 5. I have reliable information that you were on your way to meet an emissary of Operator 5 here in Denver, when you were captured. That emissary is the woman, Diane Elliot."

Rudolph leaned forward in his chair, the veins suddenly standing out on his forehead. "Randall, I would give half my empire to capture Operator 5, or the Elliot girl. Do you think I will stop at anything to make you talk? *Where is she hiding?*"

Randall looked away from the Emperor, spat deliberately on the floor, then returned his gaze to Rudolph. "Go to hell!" he said very calmly.

Rudolph's hands clenched upon the arms of his chair. He jerked his head at the executioner. "Go ahead, Balku!"

The huge, brutish-faced man sighed deeply, and a grin of almost devilish delight spread over his countenance. He shuffled forward toward the bound man, swinging his wicked club. **RANDALL PRESSED** his body erect, and gazed defiantly at the executioner. Not a muscle of his face twitched as he saw that deadly club rise in the air, with its grisly spiked ball on the end. But his eyes watched it fascinatedly.

Balku came to within a foot of him, raised the club and brought it down in a short, sharp blow upon Randall's left shoulder. The blow was not a very hard one, for Balku's technique was to increase the pain and punishment step by step until the victim could no longer bear up under the intolerable torture.

However, though the blow was not a hard one, the iron spikes tore the skin on Randall's shoulder, leaving three large blobs of redness where the blood spurted.

Almost at once, Balku raised his club and brought it down again on the same spot, this time a good deal harder. Randall winced. The spikes sank into his flesh all the way, and there was a dull, crunching sound as the body of the iron ball thudded against bone.

Randall swallowed hard, and perspiration beaded his forehead even heavier than before. But he did not utter a sound. With compressed lips he stared straight into the executioner's bestial face.

Balku grinned, twisted the spiked ball wickedly, and yanked it out.

Blood began to flow freely now, streaming down Randall's body.

Balku stepped back, turned and bowed to Rudolph.

Rudolph nodded to him approvingly, then spoke to Randall. "Well? Are you ready to talk?"

Randall was making a game effort to hide the agony he felt.

Rudolph's eyes were eagerly devouring the victim's face for some sign of surrender. "We can go on and on like this," he said. "Balku will cover every inch of your body with the spikes. He will gradually break all the small bones, and then the large ones. Then you will be thrown out into the street. Is it not better to talk?"

Randall spat crimson on the floor. "Go to hell!" he repeated.

Rudolph studied him carefully, with a little wonder in his glance.

Balku stepped to the Emperor's side. "Shall I go on, master? I will make him cringe. I will make him scream. I will make him beg to talk—"

"No, no!" Rudolph interrupted. "These Americans are strange men. They seem to be willing to die for their honor. I believe that this man would let every bone in his body be broken, and still not talk!"

"Then what shall I do, master?"

Rudolph's eyes were wily, cunning. "Randall's wife is among our prisoners, is she not?"

"Yes, master. But there are thirty or forty women prisoners, and we cannot tell which is which. The captain of the guard thinks that they have not given their own names."

"I think we can soon fix that," the Emperor said. His eyes were twinkling weirdly. "Randall's wife knows all the plans of the Americans. She has been helping him to recruit. If we cannot make Randall talk, we will have more success with his wife!"

"But how will you find her, master? We cannot tell which one—"

Rudolph laughed harshly. "We will find her!"

He rang a bell upon a small table at his side, and at once a trooper entered in answer.

"You will tell the captain of the Guard," Rudolph instructed the trooper, "to bring here all the women prisoners who were taken yesterday. I want every one of them here, at once!" The trooper saluted, and left.

RANDALL, STILL standing erect against his cross, with the blood streaming from his wounded shoulder, watched Rudolph closely. There was a shadow of anxiety in his eyes. The Emperor and his pet executioner had talked too low for him to hear, but he knew that his wife was among those women prisoners, and it bothered him. What deviltry was the sadistic Emperor up to now?

Rudolph must have read his mind. "You are wondering what is going to happen, are you not?"

Randall did not answer.

Rudolph chuckled. "You shall soon see, my friend!"

A deep, ominous silence descended upon this chamber of horror. While the three men waited, no sound was heard, except for the wheezy breathing of Balku. In the cells behind the cross to which he was tied, Randall knew that there were forty or fifty other men, awaiting their turn to be tortured, broken by this brute executioner and his devilish master. But nothing could be heard from those cells, for they were closed off from the world by heavy oak doors. No light and sound could penetrate through those doors; and the men within them had become living cadavers, existing miserably in solitude, often welcoming even the temporary release from their cells when their turn came to be subjected to the tender mercies of Balku.

The worst crime that these men had committed was that they

had fought for their country's freedom. And they were paying an awful price for their daring.

The room remained thus in utter silence for perhaps ten minutes, until the shuffling of many feet in the corridor outside announced the arrival of the women prisoners. These women had been captured, together with Randall, as the result of an intercepted message. The message had been sent by carrier pigeon,* and the pigeon had been shot down by a Purple trooper. The message was being carried to Randall, and notified him that his wife was safe, having taken refuge with some forty other women, in an abandoned excavation outside of Denver.

The sender of the message had been careless enough to put the information in writing; and those women were now paying the penalty of another's mistake. They were all the wives of active leaders of local groups throughout this section. And since the

---

* AUTHOR'S NOTE: The reader must realize that at this time, carrier pigeons and smoke signals and semaphores were about the only means of transmitting messages. The destruction inflicted upon the country by the dreadful war of invasion was widespread. Telephone wires were down everywhere, and even if they had remained up, the telephones could not have been operated because almost every means of converting power into electrical energy had been destroyed. The country—friend and foe alike—was reduced to the most primitive means of existence; and this was certainly not out of accord with the primitive nature of the conquerors and their Emperor, who indulged in every lust and passion that civilized man had succeeded in burying beneath a veneer of culture and restraint.

Purple espionage department could not reach these men, they were going to punish the wives.

Randall had not known that his wife was a prisoner. Now as he hung upon the torture rack, with his shoulder bleeding profusely, his eyes strayed over the women prisoners as they were herded into the room; and suddenly he stiffened, almost immediately repressing the start of astonishment at sight of his wife among them.

He glanced toward Rudolph, and saw that the Emperor had been watching him carefully.

Rudolph said to him softly, "One of these women is your wife, eh, Randall?"

Randall shook his head. His shoulder was throbbing with a dull, burning pain.

"No!" he said.

But he had seen her. Elsie Randall, slim, slight of build, with a shawl over her head, was in the first rank of those women. For a fleeting instant her eyes met those of her husband, and she raised a hand to her breast. Her lips trembled. She saw her husband's bloody shoulder, and realized what it meant.

RUDOLPH, SEATING himself once more in his chair, spoke to the women prisoners. "One of you," he said coldly, "is the wife of this man. She knows his secrets. I want her to step forward, and tell me where the girl, Diane Elliot, is hiding. Otherwise, she shall see her husband die—slowly and painfully!"

For a long moment, no one in the room spoke. Balku stood beside his master's chair, fondling the wicked club with the spiked ball.

The chamber, large and low-ceilinged, was lighted by two pair of huge candelabra at either end. And the candle flames flared fitfully, throwing queer shadows everywhere, illuminating the faces of the women prisoners with a strange, foreboding glow. The guards who had conducted them here stood at the doors with bayonets ready, viewing the scene with unmoved detachment.

Rudolph sat forward in his chair, staring at them, his eyes gleaming, his thickly sensuous lips twisted into a smile of vicious enjoyment.

"Well?" he asked. "Which of you is Randall's wife? Speak quickly!"

Elsie Randall shrank into herself, fearing to betray her identity by so much as a single motion. The other women dared not glance at her, for fear of betraying her. And Joseph Randall's muscles tightened as he hung upon the rack. His face was set hard as granite, his mouth a tight line of bitterness.

Rudolph shifted impatiently in his seat. "So," he said softly. He turned to the executioner. "Proceed, Balku. It would seem that Mrs. Randall, whoever she is, wishes to see her husband die. Show her, Balku—show her!"

Balku licked his lips, stepped forward. Randall's eyes were fixed upon him now in fearful fascination. He could have borne the prospect of being broken into a bloody pulp by this brute. But that his wife should be forced to be a witness was asking almost too much of any man.

He gritted his teeth, waited tautly as Balku stepped close, grinning. The executioner raised his spiked club, allowed it to remain poised in the air for a moment, then brought it down hard, smashing its iron spikes squarely against Randall's bare chest.

The skin broke as the spikes gouged into his flesh. Blood spurted in little geysers. Randall barely restrained a groan. Balku tore the spiked ball away, raised it and brought it down again. Three, four, five times he struck, in quick succession, making a gory line across the prisoner's chest. And the fourth time, Randall groaned aloud.

Balku grinned, glanced at the Emperor, who nodded.

Balku stepped back a pace, viewing his handiwork with satisfaction, Randall's body was covered with streaming blood now, and his face was white as chalk. Only his eyes burned with live hatred at Rudolph and Balku. His body twitched with the agony of those spike-wounds.

Rudolph uttered a short, high-pitched laugh.

"Well, Mrs. Randall? Do you wish to see more?"

The women prisoners, huddled together, seemed frozen into terrified silence. Elsie Randall stared down at the floor, not daring to look at her husband's tortured body.

Randall, straining at the bonds that tied him to the rack, called out in an agonized voice, "No, no, Elsie. Don't talk, for God's sake!"

Rudolph laughed again. He raised a hand to the executioner.

"More, Balku!" he said softly. Balku bowed, stepped forward once more, with his bloody spiked club raised.

And that was too much for Elsie Randall. Suddenly, frenzied words poured from her lips in a wild torrent.

"Stop! Stop! For the love of God, don't torture him any more! I'll tell you what you want to know. Only spare him!"

She stepped out from the group of women, her arms raised in supplication.

Joseph Randall groaned, and closed his eyes. "You shouldn't have done it, Elsie," he murmured.

Elsie Randall went to him impulsively, put a trembling hand upon the raw wounds in his chest. "Darling, I—I couldn't see you suffer so!"

Rudolph smiled smugly.

"Speak quickly, Mrs. Randall. Where is Diane Elliot?"

Elsie Randall turned to him, her lips trembling. "She—she is hiding—in the barn of the old farmhouse just outside the Curtis Aviation Field!" She drooped suddenly, and closed her eyes. "God forgive me for what I have just done!"

RUDOLPH'S EYES were gleaming with triumph. A deep sigh escaped his lips. He motioned to the sergeant in charge of the guards. "Notify the captain of the guard to send a detail of men to the farmhouse near the Curtis Aviation Field. He is to arrest everyone there. If he fails to find the Elliot girl, I will have him flayed alive!"

He rose from his chair. "Take the women away. Keep Mrs. Randall separate from the others. And take Randall back to his cell."

The Emperor turned to his executioner. "Come, Balku. You have done well. We are through here for the present. You must prepare the cage in the courtyard, for your jaguar. We shall have a guest for the cage shortly!"

He started for the door, while the guards began to herd the women to one side.

And it was at that moment that an orderly entered the room. The man saluted, then bowed low. "Your Imperial Majesty! The Americans are raiding the city! They have attacked the Imperial Concentration Camp, and they are marching on the palace!"

Rudolph's eyes narrowed. "How many of them are there?"

"Only five or six hundred, Your Majesty. But the civilians are joining them in droves. There will be thousands soon."

"Hah! We shall stop that quickly. Go at once to Colonel von Sturm. Order him to turn out the garrison!"

"It is already done, Your Majesty. The troops are massing about the palace. There is much street fighting, but Colonel von Sturm reports that he believes he can control the uprising."

"Good. Come, Balku. We must prepare to receive the Elliot girl!"

He strode from the room, smiling.

As he mounted the stairs to the upper floors of the building, with Balku close behind him, he could begin to hear the sounds of shooting from the southern section of the city. In the corridors there was a good deal of commotion, with messengers and orderlies hastening with messages for the garrison.

Rudolph saw Captain Kiel, the captain of the Guard, marching toward the doorway at the head of a detail of ten men. The captain came to a halt, saluted briskly.

Rudolph nodded to him. "You received my orders from the sergeant."

Captain Kiel bowed. "Yes, Your Majesty. I am on my way to arrest the Elliot girl."

"See that you do not fail. I hear there is fighting in the city. Take more men. You must allow nothing to interfere with you. If you meet any opposition, you must have enough men to smash it. I want that Elliot girl!"

The captain saluted. "I shall take more men on the way, Your Majesty."

Rudolph waved him on, and proceeded down the corridor into the main room, which faced upon the spacious grounds, and which he had converted into an audience chamber. Several officers who were awaiting him here, stood to attention as he entered, and a very beautiful, dark-haired woman stepped toward him, smiling.

Rudolph nodded to her. "I am glad to see that you are feeling well again, Anita. You look more beautiful now every day!"

If Rudolph's eyes had been cruel, sadistic before, they now showed a miraculous change. They seemed to devour this beautiful woman whom the Emperor had called Anita. They became hot, possessive.

This was the Baroness Anita Monfred, the one person in the world who was able to evoke in the Emperor's breast a feeling other than hatred or cruelty. He intended some day to make her the empress of the world—whether she liked it or not. And it was an ironical twist of circumstance that Baroness Anita Monfred, who could have the love of the most powerful emperor in the history of the world, should have fallen in love, herself, with the Emperor's most hated enemy. But it was true. Anita

Monfred had once offered herself to Operator 5. And Jimmy Christopher had refused her love.*

Rudolph had been glad to pardon her upon her return to court, for she was perhaps the only being in the world for whom he entertained any degree of affection.

NOW, THE Emperor led Anita Monfred across the room to the window. Here they were afforded a view of Cheesman Park,

---

* AUTHOR'S NOTE: Those readers who have followed the history of the Purple Invasion will recall Anita Monfred. In the early days of the invasion she was constantly at the Emperor's side often helping to soothe his ungovernable flashes of rage and temper. She had at one time been instrumental in capturing Operator 5; but had fallen in love with him with all the fierceness of which she was capable. One day when he was a prisoner in New York, condemned to die the next day, she had come to him and offered him escape—and herself. Operator 5, deeply in love with Diane Elliot, infuriated her by failing to respond to her offer. He could not bring himself even to touch this woman who was destined to became the wife of Rudolph I—and he could not understand how so beautiful a creature could resign herself to living with such a man. Anita Monfred, realizing that Operator 5 loved Diane Elliot, aided Operator 5 to escape anyway, thereby incurring the Emperor's displeasure. She was forced to flee from the court, and sought refuge with the American army. Subsequently, the Emperor pardoned her, and she returned to court. But there still rankled in her breast the memory of the night when Operator 5, a prisoner condemned to die, had refused her love even at the price of his life. Whether, at this time, she still loved Operator 5, it is difficult to say. But it is not strange that she should be eager to aid in the capture of the man who had spurned her.

as well as of a good deal of the city to the south. They could see the massed companies of Purple troops wheeling into formation to meet the expected attack of the Americans, and they could also see spurts of smoke and hear the crackling of musketry far to the south where the fighting was taking place.

Anita Monfred turned from the window to the Emperor. "The Americans must be very desperate to do this at a time when we have so many troops in the city," she said.

Rudolph nodded. "Either they are desperate, Anita, or they have a very good plan—and good leadership!"

Her eyes narrowed. "You mean—"

"I mean"—Rudolph's mouth tightened into a thin line of cruelty—"that Operator 5 must be the leader of this raid. No one else would have the courage."

The courtiers and officers in the room stood at respectful attention while the Emperor and Anita Monfred conversed at the window in low tones.

The baroness was silent for a moment, digesting what Rudolph had just said. At last she spoke. "You—think that Operator 5 may be successful?"

Rudolph shrugged. "I hate him, but I do not underestimate him. He would not undertake such a raid, unless he had a fair chance of succeeding. It may be that he has incited the countryside to rise against us. In that case, he might prove dangerous."

"Is there anything we can do to stop him?"

Rudolph said slowly, "Yes."

The baroness glanced at him queerly. "You have a plan?"

"I have. I would need your help."

BALKU
THE
EXECUTIONER

GENERAL
SHAN HI MUNG

BARON FLEXNER

"I will give it gladly. Nothing would please me more than to see Operator 5 in your power."

"There was a time when you did not think so. In fact, you even helped him to escape."

"That is over!" Anita Monfred exclaimed fiercely. Her eyes flashed fire. "I would do anything to destroy that man!"

BARONESS
ANITA
MONFRED

RUDOLPH

The Emperor chuckled. "You are a strange woman, Anita. Perhaps that is why I care for you so deeply. One day you can love, and the next day you can hate as fiercely. See that you never come to hate me like that!"

Anita Monfred stirred impatiently. "Never mind that. Tell me what you want done."

"Very good. Operator 5 still trusts you? He still thinks you friendly to him?"

"Yes. I never let him know how I felt."

"Excellent. You will go to him. Go to the southern portion of the city, and contact the American column. Tell them that you have important information for Operator 5."

"And when I reach him?"

"You will tell him that his fiancée, Diane Elliot, is a prisoner of mine. You will tell him that tonight she is to be placed in the great cage outside this palace, with a live jaguar."

Anita Monfred started perceptibly. "Is this true?" she asked huskily.

"It is true. I have just learned where Diane Elliot is hiding. Within an hour, she will be here. The captain of the Guard has gone to arrest her!"

Anita Monfred's countenance became convulsed with passion for a brief instant. She hated Diane, who had been able to hold Jimmy Christopher in spite of the baroness's every alluring effort. It would be a supreme triumph for her to see Diane Elliot placed in the cage with the jaguar, while Operator 5 stood by, a helpless prisoner, unable to rescue his fiancée.

"I want to be sure to be present," she said throatily, "when the jaguar buries his claws in the Elliot girl's throat!"

"You shall see it, Anita, I promise you," Rudolph told her. "But you must bring Operator 5 here for us to capture."

"How shall I do that?"

"You will tell Operator 5 that you cannot bear to think of Diane Elliot being clawed to death by the jaguar. You will offer to help him rescue her. Tell him that since you know the password of the day, you can guide him back into the palace here, through our lines. You will say that the delivery entrance on the north side of the building is lightly guarded, by only a single sentry. Take him to that entrance, and when you get there, the rest will be taken care of!"

Anita Monfred's smile was one of high satisfaction. "I will do it, Rudolph—now!"

He nodded. "Go, Anita. Bring me Operator 5, and you shall have every reward that I have promised for his capture!"

The baroness turned and went swiftly from the room.

To the north, as Emperor Rudolph I looked out through the window, the firing had grown in volume, indicating that the main body of Purple troops had come into contact with the Americans. Rudolph swung to his officers, gave swift orders.

"Send strong detachments of troops to guard every approach to the city. The American guerrillas will be flocking in here soon, to help their friends. We must not allow them to enter. If we can keep all help from reaching Operator 5 and his men here in the city, we should be able to destroy them!"

A staff officer saluted, and withdrew.

To another officer, Rudolph rapped, "Send a pigeon to Marshal Kremer, in command of the front lines at the Continental Divide. Instruct him to erect crosses in front of our trenches, and to tie to those crosses all the American prisoners whom we have sent him. When the Americans advance to attack, they will not be able to shoot unless they are willing to kill their own people!"

He grinned thinly. "I promised that the first-born would be crucified. Well, I'll let the Americans execute their own first born if they persist in attacking. That is a little trick that no general has ever thought of before, eh?"

With a touch of pride, he twirled his carefully trimmed imperial mustache, and smiled with smug satisfaction. Soon all opposition promised to be eliminated. With the American Defense Force stopped at the Continental Divide, with Operator 5 a prisoner slated for painful death, all signs pointed to the complete and speedy submission of the American people. In a way, Rudolph I was glad that Operator 5 had staged this raid in Denver today!

He began to laugh.

CHAPTER 7
THE LIVING WALL

THE FIGHTING in the streets of Denver had settled down to a steady exchange of musketry fire between barricaded troops. Jimmy Christopher, in charge of operations, with his headquarters at the concentration camp, realized that his woefully small force could not hope to storm the Imperial Palace in the face of the two additional brigades of infantry which Rudolph had in the city. But if he could only hold the ground he had gained so far, the situation might change by nightfall.

In the first place, the word was going out throughout the countryside that Operator 5 had struck, and American volunteers would be hurrying toward Denver from every direction. In the second place, zero hour for the American attack along the far-flung battle line at the Continental Divide was set for six o'clock that evening, and when the Americans under General Hank Sheridan went over the top, the Purple High Command would need every available reserve there. The problem, however, was how to hold out till nightfall. He had eight hundred men. Six hundred of these were already engaged with the enemy. Here at the concentration camp, though, American civilians were thronging about the supply wagons, being provided with guns and ammunition as fast as Tim Donovan and the scouts could possibly hand them out. Every civilian in the city had learned through that strange underground grapevine that exists in every conquered country, that Operator 5 was at the concentration camp, looking for recruits. And those civilians left their wives and families at home, to make their way circuitously, ducking through back streets to avoid the moving Purple troops, until they reached the camp. Many brought their own arms, which they had kept concealed, as MacPherson had done, until the day came to strike. Others got their weapons from the stores taken out of the captured barracks building.

Operator 5's eyes glowed with pride as he saw company after company of fresh volunteers form in the square and march toward the palace under the command of MacPherson's men. Only a short distance away, where the first contingent of Americans had met the Purple troops, the battle was being fought hotly.

Operator 5's foresightedness in ordering barricades thrown up was rewarded now. The Americans were able to take shelter behind those barricades, and volley after volley drove back the advancing Purple infantry. The banks of Cherry Creek became a shambles as attack after attack was driven back, the Purple forces leaving their dead in the street.

Frank MacPherson sent back word by runner that he wanted permission to resume his advance, but Jimmy Christopher would not allow it.

"Tell Mac," he instructed the messenger, "that all we want to do is hold our ground till evening. We'll advance after nightfall. We can't afford to do it now, because we're not strong enough."

He paced up and down in front of the gate, scowling at the enforced inaction. From where he stood he could look up along Cherry Creek and see the barricades where Frank MacPherson's men were holding the enemy. On either side of him, to the east and the west, other sections of the American volunteers were waiting, prepared to repel any flank attacks which might be launched against them. To the rear, at the far end of the concentration camp, still others waited behind the barbed-wire in the event of an attack from the rear.

Jimmy Christopher had planned this engagement well. Entrenched as they were now, and with the food supplies from the concentration camp at their disposal, they could hold the enemy off for a long time. The only approach available to the Purple troops was along the streets which the Americans had barricaded, and in those streets the enemy's numerical superiority was not a major factor.

JIMMY, HIMSELF, longed to be at the barricades, active in the fighting, instead of merely directing operations. Long ago, in the early days of the invasion, his genius for strategy had been clearly demonstrated, and he could have had supreme command of the American Defense Force had he wanted it.

But he was not the type to seek an executive position when there was fighting to be done. He had urged the supreme command upon Hank Sheridan, and contented himself with lending advice and counsel. General Sheridan, although not originally trained for warfare, had done very well considering the handicaps against him. And it was General Hank Sheridan who was tonight to direct the American offensive.

Operator 5 gazed somberly toward the west, disregarding utterly stray bullets from the battle, which occasionally *pinged* into the barbed-wire behind him.

If he could make this raid strong enough, if he could only succeed in capturing Rudolph I, Hank Sheridan's task at the Continental Divide would be greatly simplified.

At this time, Jimmy Christopher knew that Rudolph planned to execute the firstborn of every American family if the drive took place at the scheduled hour; but he did not know of Rudolph's fiendishly diabolical order to place the captives upon crosses in front of the Purple trenches.

Now, as he paced up and down impatiently, Tim Donovan came over to him from the supply wagon. Tim was flushed with excitement, and grinning happily.

"Boy, this is what I call action!" the freckle-faced lad exclaimed. "We've handed out fifteen hundred guns and enough rounds of ammunition to keep them going all day. Boy, that barracks building was sure a gold mine!"

Jimmy smiled at him soberly, but said nothing.

Tim Donovan became instantly solicitous. "What's up, Jimmy? You look worried."

"I am, Tim. It's about Diane. With this fighting going on, she'll be stranded at that farm house where we were supposed to contact her. She had all the carrier pigeons ready to send out to the local leaders instructing them to make their attacks simultaneously at six o'clock tonight. But she wasn't to send them off until we arrived there. I hope when she hears the battle, she'll understand what's happened, and loose the pigeons."

"Don't worry, Jimmy, she will. You can always depend on Di to do the right thing! Haven't you heard from the men that George MacPherson sent out to contact her?"

Jimmy shook his head. He pointed toward the north, where a sudden spurt of fresh fighting had broken out. "There's the first flank attack. The Purple troops probably have us entirely surrounded by this time. No one could get through."

"Gee, Jimmy," Tim Donovan said thoughtfully, "we've got about twenty-five hundred men with the new recruits. If the Purple troops have us surrounded, it must be taking every available soldier in the garrison."

"That's what I want, Tim. I want them to concentrate on us, and leave the approaches to the city clear, so that the volunteers from the countryside can march in. Then Rudolph will have to send for more troops from the front to quell the uprising, and he'll weaken Marshal Kremer's effectiveness at the Continental Divide. If Diane has sent out her pigeons, and the same thing happens in a hundred cities in the Occupied Territory, it would give Hank Sheridan a great advantage."

Tim Donovan nodded his approval. "That's swell stuff, Jimmy. It ought to work."

"It *has* to work," Jimmy said grimly. "It's our last effort. If this push fails, America will be thoroughly licked." He paused, and pointed toward the north. "Here comes Frank MacPherson, riding like the devil. I wonder what's the trouble."

THE ONE-ARMED scout leader was spurring his horse toward them from the direction of the barricades, riding as skillfully with his one hand as most men with two. When he reached them he dismounted, and spoke swiftly. "Look here, Operator 5, I want you to let me move forward. There's only a comparatively small number of Purple troops in front of us. If we advance up Cherry Creek, we can reach the Imperial Palace. The creek runs past the State Building, only a few hundred yards to the west. We have a good chance of surrounding the building and capturing Rudolph!"

Jimmy shook his head in the negative. "It won't do, Mac. We haven't enough men to surround the palace. Our best bet is to keep the troops occupied so they'll leave the approaches to the city free, as I was just telling Tim. We have a good spot here, and we can hold out all day. And—"

He paused, staring at two individuals who had suddenly appeared, riding toward them from the south. One was a woman, the other was young George MacPherson.

Both Tim Donovan and Jimmy Christopher recognized the woman. Tim exclaimed, "Gee, Jimmy, it's Anita Monfred!"

Operator 5 nodded, his forehead furrowed in perplexity. "She's as beautiful as ever—and as dangerous!"

They waited while the two riders approached. George MacPherson dismounted, and then helped the Baroness Anita off her horse. Anita was carrying a small package under her arm. She stood silently, looking at Jimmy Christopher with eyes that had suddenly become veiled depths of hidden meaning.

George MacPherson was the first to speak. "You know the Baroness Anita Monfred, Operator 5?"

Jimmy Christopher nodded. "What brings you to the enemy lines, Anita?" he asked.

She stepped forward, spoke impulsively. "Operator 5, I have very bad news for you. Your—friend, Diane Elliot, has been captured by the Emperor's men!"

Jimmy started, his eyes narrowing. "You can prove this?"

George MacPherson broke in, soberly. "It's true, Operator 5. I went to the farmhouse near the airport to contact Miss Elliot, and I found the Purple troops there ahead of me. They were leading Miss Elliot away, and they had set fire to the farmhouse. There were too many men for me to attack, so I hurried back. The only way to get through the enemy lines was in the west side of the city. I met the baroness there, and she asked me to take her to you."

Anita Monfred said impulsively, with every appearance of sincerity: "As soon as I heard that Miss Elliot was captured, I decided to come to you, Operator 5. They are going to do a terrible thing to her. They are going to put her in a cage with Balku's pet jaguar. She'll be clawed to death. I—I couldn't bear to think of her meeting such a fate. I—I'm going to help you to save her, Operator 5!"

"How?" Jimmy asked dryly.

Eagerly, she opened the package she was carrying, revealing a complete field uniform of a colonel of Imperial Purple Hussars.

"If you will put this on, I can guide you through our lines, into the palace. The delivery door on the north side is not well guarded. You can overpower the sentry, and get into the dungeons downstairs. When you rescue Miss Elliot, I'll have horses waiting at the north door, and you will ride."

She paused, looked at him coyly. "You see, Operator 5, I—I am still silly enough to want to see you happy!"

JIMMY GAZED at her for a long time, studying her. There was nothing in Anita's attitude to indicate what her inner feelings might be. But he knew her well enough from the past, to understand that she was hardly the type of person to help Diane to escape. Rather, she would aid to destroy her.

He looked at her silently, and she returned his gaze steadily. At last he said, "I'll go with you, Anita."

She smiled. "I thought you would!"

Tim Donovan plucked at Jimmy's sleeve. "Come here a minute. I want to talk to you in private. You, too, Mr. MacPherson." His manner was secretive.

Old MacPherson and Jimmy Christopher followed the lad a few feet away, out of earshot of the baroness.

Tim Donovan faced the two men, but addressed Operator 5, speaking earnestly. "Look here, Jimmy, I don't trust that dame for two cents' worth. Maybe it's true that Diane is captured, but she isn't going to help you—she's going to lead you into a trap. I feel it in my bones!"

"The boy is right, Operator 5," Frank MacPherson broke in. "You can't afford to risk your life by going to rescue Miss Elliot. We need you too much. Don't forget that all of us have mothers and sisters and wives, and we're leaving them in their homes, at the mercy of the enemy. You've got to do the same."

Jimmy Christopher faced MacPherson, frowning. "You ought to know me better than that, Mac. If it were a question of Diane's life alone, God help me, I might leave her to die. I'm sure she'd want it that way."

He paused, turned to glance at Anita Monfred, who was watching them interestedly, and then went on: "But I've got to find out if she released those pigeons before she was captured. Don't you see, Mac, that everything depends on that? If Diane didn't have a chance to send the messages, then there won't be any general uprising in the countryside. Our whole plan will fall through. *I've got to find out if those messages were sent!*"

MacPherson lowered his eyes. "I guess you're right, Operator 5. That's important. But couldn't some one else go in your place?"

Jimmy Christopher smiled tightly. "I can't trust any one else with the job, Mac. The fate of America hangs on it. You can get along all right, here. You're barricaded pretty well, and you have men and supplies. I promise you that if Diane didn't send those messages, I'll get word out myself, somehow."

Tim Donovan held onto his sleeve, "But suppose it's a trap, Jimmy—"

"I'll have to take my chances on that, kid!"

He left them, took the bundle from Anita Monfred, and climbed into the supply wagon to change into them.

Tim Donovan, watching Anita Monfred, saw a light of fierce triumph come into her face. She turned, saw Tim looking at her, and quickly veiled her eyes.

Ten minutes later, Jimmy Christopher was ready to start with Anita Monfred. He left some last-minute instructions with MacPherson, said good-bye to Tim, and helped Anita Monfred onto her horse. He waved his hand on farewell, and they trotted off to the west.

For a moment Tim Donovan watched them riding away. Then, impulsively, he turned to Frank MacPherson. "Give me a horse!" he exclaimed. "I'm going to follow them. I don't trust that dame, and I have a hunch Jimmy's going to need some help!"

"Good kid!" MacPherson grinned. "I wish I had a friend like you!"

CHAPTER 8
ZERO HOUR FOR A NATION

O N A ridge overlooking Fremont Pass, in the heart of the Continental Divide, General Hank Sheridan stood in close consultation with his staff officers. He held his left wrist up in front of him as he talked. The waning daylight enabled him still to see the face of his wrist-watch there. That watch showed the time to be seven minutes before six o'clock.

Hank Sheridan spoke in a crisp, tight voice. "Gentlemen, it

is seven minutes before zero hour. Have you all carried out your instructions—*to the letter?*"

He gazed around at the circle of faces about him, and each of the officers nodded in turn. "Naturally," he said dryly, "there will be no barrage preceding the advance—inasmuch as we have no ammunition for the big guns. Colonel Mackenzie, have you instructed all divisional commanders to order their men to try to reach close quarters as quickly as possible?"

Colonel Mackenzie nodded. "I have, sir. Groups of snipers will advance behind each attacking contingent, and they will also be covered by concentrated rifle fire from men whom we have posted in all the ridges. The infantry have been instructed to try to come to grips with the enemy as quickly as possible, where they will be able to use cold steel."

"Good," said Hank Sheridan. "And you, Major Rowlan? You have arranged for cavalry reserves to mop up after each charge?"

"That's all been arranged, sir. The infantry have been instructed that wherever they succeed in putting the enemy to flight, they are to lay board bridges across the captured trenches so that the cavalry can sweep across in pursuit of the retreating enemy. In that way, the enemy will not be given an opportunity to reform their ranks for a second stand."

"Excellent!" General Sheridan exclaimed. He glanced at his watch. "Four and one-half minutes more, gentlemen!"

The small group of officers waited tensely, while the seconds ticked away with deadly slowness.

"The first thing we should hear at zero hour," Colonel Mackenzie said, "are the heavy rifle fire of the riflemen in the ridges, laying down a barrage upon the passes. That is scheduled to last for two minutes. Then it ceases, and the troops advance."

"I wonder," Colonel Rowlan mused, "how the men will fight. Will they have any heart for it?"

No one challenged his statement, or presumed to answer his question. Rowlan continued reflectively, "Every one of those boys has a near relative or a dear friend in the Occupied Territory. And they had all heard Rudolph's proclamation, that if the advance takes place, the first-born in each family will be crucified. Can the boys do it, knowing that they will be deliberately sentencing thousands of innocent youngsters to crucifixion?"

"I think, yes," Hank Sheridan said slowly. "Operator 5 made a promise to them before he left. He promised that if it were humanly possible, he would prevent the carrying out of that proclamation. The boys have confidence in Operator 5. And if he fails, they will know that he must be dead. I think they will be willing to make the sacrifice of their loved ones, rather than see them remain slaves of the Purple Empire for the rest of their lives!"

"We'll soon know," Major Rowlan said moodily. He glanced at his own wrist-watch. "In three and one-half minutes, to be exact."

No one spoke after that, until the minute hand of Hank Sheridan's watch reached the zenith of the dial. It was six o'clock.

Zero hour!

A deep sigh escaped from all the officers in the small group. They tautened, waiting for the first sounds of musketry fire that would announce the beginning of the battle.

As from a great distance, a few rifle shots sounded, barking dismally in the fast-falling dusk. But they were only sporadic shots, and not the heavy firing that a rifle-barrage would have required.

A frown appeared upon Hank Sheridan's forehead. Colonel Mackenzie, Major Rowlan, and the other officers all turned to stare to the east, where Fremont Pass lay before them. Hank Sheridan raised a pair of field glasses, focused them on the pass. He could clearly see the enemy trenches dug across the pass, could see the figures of the Americans advancing toward those trenches. But something had clearly gone wrong, for there should have been two minutes of rifle fire before the advance.

And now he shuddered as he saw what must be the reason for the lack of rifle fire. Strung across the front of the enemy trenches, where they would be directly in the line of fire, were dozens upon dozens of wooden crosses, upon which were tied human beings.

And though the Americans were advancing without firing a single shot, the Purple troopers were shooting freely, mowing the advancing Americans down cruelly.

HANK SHERIDAN'S mouth tightened into a thin line. He took down his glasses, and faced the other officers. At that moment a breathless messenger came running from the heliograph station at the crest of the ridge.

"We've just got a message from Captain Mutrie, sir, at the front lines. He reports that the Purple troops have suddenly put up crosses in front of their trenches. And American boys and girls are tied to those crosses. If we fire, we'll surely kill our own children!"

Colonel Mackenzie swore feelingly. "By God, I'd like to have that Rudolph's neck inside these two hands of mine for just two minutes!"

Hank Sheridan had raised his glass once more, and a grim smile appeared on his lips. "Look, gentlemen," he said. "Those crosses aren't stopping the boys!"

It was true. The American troops were advancing in the face of the withering fire from the trenches, and yet they refrained, themselves, from firing a single shot. Hank Sheridan saw them fall by the hundreds, but others took their places, advanced grimly, with bayonets fixed to their rifles, with swords, scythes, whatever weapons they carried.

They were giving their answer to Rudolph's uncanny cruelty!

Hank Sheridan sighed. His eyes were wet, and he blinked hard.

"I—I think, gentlemen, that we will yet have victory!"

He kept his glass focused on the pass below, while every few moments fresh messages arrived, informing him that another sector had been taken by the Americans.

And as he watched, the Americans advancing in Fremont Pass finally reached the enemy trench, losing hundreds of men in the charge. But they went over the breastworks, and Hank Sheridan was grim as he watched bayonets rise and fall with deadly speed. The Americans were exacting payment for those children that had been placed on the crosses. They were giving no quarter.

At last Hank Sheridan turned to Major Rowlan. "I think, Major, that you can order the cavalry to move up...."*

IN THE city of Denver, fighting had been going on all day. The Americans barricaded in the streets leading to the captured concentration camp kept the enemy garrison busy, as did the numerous contingents of volunteers arriving from the countryside. Americans were pouring in by every road, and there was fighting in almost every street.

The fighting was grim, deadly, bloody. As fresh groups of Americans arrived, the Purple commanders were forced to draw off company after company from the fighting around the concentration camp, to send to other parts of the city. And as a result, George MacPherson was enabled to advance his men closer to the State Building where he knew Rudolph to be.

Every inch of the ground was fought bitterly, and MacPherson lost many men with each block gained, because he had to bring them out from behind the protection of the barricades. But

---

* AUTHOR'S NOTE: The historian, Harrison Stievers, in his monumental work, *The History of the Purple War*, informs us that no less than *seven thousand* of those sinister black crosses were erected in front of the enemy trenches at the Battle of the Continental Divide. Thus, seven thousand youngsters, ranging in age from five to eighteen years, were exposed to American fire. And it is significant that not one of those youngsters was killed or wounded by an American bullet. But it is just as significant that fully fifteen hundred of those poor children *were shot in the back* by the Purple troops as they fled in defeat. No wonder then, that the Americans showed no mercy, gave no quarter, when they took a trench!

as evening drew on, his men fought with refreshed vigor, as if they had been given a new lease on strength; for they knew that this was zero hour for every American in the country, whether he was with the American Defense Force at the Continental Divide, or whether he was a civilian in the Occupied Territory.

And MacPherson himself was anxious to reach the palace for another reason. Strange stories had filtered through to him, of a huge cage erected in the courtyard in front of the palace, with a live, deadly jaguar in it. He remembered the story that Anita Monfred had brought of the capture of Diane Elliot. He might have placed little credence in that story, had it not been corroborated by his own son. And he was worried about Operator 5. He was almost sure that Jimmy Christopher had walked into a trap with the Monfred woman.

He urged his men on with redoubled fierceness, and little by little they fought their way along Cherry Creek toward the State Building which they could see now, across miles of debris and ruins. The fighting became more intense as additional Purple troops were thrown into the streets along Cherry Creek to stem the advance of the determined Americans.

Meanwhile, in the palace grounds, a strange scene was being enacted.

The spacious grounds fronting on Cheesman Park had been converted into a military parade ground with the occupation of the city by the Purple Emperor. Now, the grounds were illuminated by dozens of torches, flaming in the hands of guards who had temporarily put aside their carbines to act as torch bearers.

Upon the steps of the palace, once the home of the governor

of the Centennial State, a dais had been erected, to accommodate the throne of Emperor Rudolph I. He sat here now, smugly
content with the entertainment he had planned, surrounded
by fawning officers and courtiers. None of these people paid
any attention to the sounds of brisk fighting going on in every
section of the city. They felt reasonably safe, in the presence of
two brigades of troops in addition to the garrison, and consid-
ered it only a matter of time before the impudent Americans
would be slaughtered to the last man.

Now, their eyes were all fixed upon the spectacle in the courtyard.

A huge cage had been erected here, with iron bars perhaps
fourteen inches apart. The cage was the size of a large room, and
there was a door to it at one side. Within this cage there paced
a huge, gaunt jaguar whose eyes gleamed in the night in the
reflection of the countless torches. Men with long poles stood
at intervals along the bars and prodded the jaguar.

The animal was becoming more infuriated by the minute,
and the Emperor and his courtiers laughed with glee each time
it growled.

NEAR THE door of the cage, two troopers stood guard over
the slender figure of Diane Elliot. She stood slim, erect, defiant, not even looking at the caged jaguar, though she knew she
was destined to be thrown to that animal within a few minutes.
Her chestnut hair shone darkly in the torchlight. They had not
bothered to bind her, thinking that it would be more amusing
to afford her an opportunity to defend herself against the jaguar
with her bare hands.

Rudolph, seated in his throne-like chair, let his eyes feast on her hungrily, in search of some slight tremor or indication that she felt fear at the thing that was going to happen to her.

But he turned at last in disgust to his executioner, who stood at his left.

"Damn these Americans, Balku!" he exclaimed petulantly. "They never show fear! What are they made of, anyhow?"

Balku shrugged. "Wait, master. When she is in the cage with the jaguar, she will be different."

Rudolph sulked. "Well, why don't we start?" He turned to a tall, suave man at his right. "What are we waiting for, Flexner?"

Baron Flexner bowed. "We are waiting for word from the Baroness Anita Monfred, your Majesty. You recall that she promised to bring Operator 5 here."

Baron Julian Flexner was Rudolph's Prime Minister. He had guided the affairs of state for his master for almost six months now, a longer period than that of any other prime minister— which spoke excellently for his diplomacy and tact.

Now, however, Rudolph was not pleased by him. "You are a fool, Flexner!" he barked. "We can go ahead with this anyway—"

"But, Your Majesty, suppose Operator 5 arrives after the Elliot girl is dead? He will have warning that he is betrayed—"

"I say go ahead!" the Emperor snapped.

Flexner shrugged, turned reluctantly to give the order. His heart was not in this business. All his skill and cleverness was at the service of the Emperor, and he had helped to plan many a cruel stroke against America. But recently something had happened which had changed the very nature of Baron Julian

101

Flexner. His own daughter, a beautiful fifteen-year-old girl, had been captured by Jimmy Christopher and Tim Donovan. They had treated her royally, and had returned her to her father unharmed. Little Freda Flexner had learned much about Americans from Tim; and upon her return she expressed her opinion of her father and of the Emperor in no uncertain terms. Previously, she had been taught that Americans were nothing but animals, not deserving or understanding anything but the most extreme cruelty. She hated her father for so misleading her, and Baron Flexner was beginning to think that it was as important to preserve a daughter's love as to serve an Emperor.

So that now he would much rather not have been entrusted with the duty of carrying out this orgy of cruelty. But he could only obey.

He raised his hand, and the troopers guarding Diane Elliot saluted, and led her toward the door of the cage. It seemed the end.

IT WAS just about at this time that Jimmy Christopher and Anita Monfred were approaching the palace from the south. Jimmy Christopher was dressed in the uniform of Captain of Imperial Hussars, which Anita Monfred had brought him. He was watchful, suspicious, as he guided his horse after hers along the path through the mangled remains of Cheesman Park. They had taken a circuitous route through the city in approaching the palace, so as to avoid the fighting, but they had nevertheless met several bodies of Purple troops on the way; and Jimmy's suspicions had been somewhat allayed, though not altogether lulled, by the fact that Anita had done nothing to betray him to

DIANE

these troops. He began to think that she was really sincere in her desire to help rescue Diane.

Nevertheless, he remained constantly alert.

Now, as the huge bulk of the palace loomed before them, Anita turned in her saddle and spoke to him. "They are preparing the cage with the jaguar on the other side of the building, Operator 5. You can see the flares of the torches. We will have to hurry before they take Miss Elliot out of her cell. Once she is in the square out there, it will be impossible to do anything to save her. There are two machine guns placed in the corner rooms on the first floor, overlooking the courtyard, and there will be more than two hundred of the Imperial household troops out there. Let us hurry."

Jimmy nodded, and made sure that his revolver slid easily in its holster. He spurred his horse closer behind hers, following her until they were almost at the wall of the building. It was quiet here, suggesting that Anita had told the truth when she said that this side of the building was not as well guarded as the other.

At a sign from the baroness they dismounted, leaving their horses tethered to a tree stump, and proceeded on foot along the wall, until they came to the small delivery door.

The night was lively with the sounds of fighting. The crackling of musketry stabbed through the night continuously from the direction of Cherry Creek, interspersed with the occasional drumming of a machine gun. Neither side was using machine guns with much freedom, for the factories capable of manufacturing cartridges for the rapid-firers were out of commission, and it was necessary to conserve the present supply of ammunition.

But Jimmy could tell by the rifle fire that the battle was growing hotter. He wished that he were back at the barricades, fighting beside the MacPhersons, or back at the Continental Divide, with Hank Sheridan. He glanced at his watch. Six o'clock. Zero hour. The boys at the Continental Divide would be going over the top right now. And men throughout the country would be rising in the last great effort for freedom. And here, if he were lucky, he might be able to strike the single blow that would help more than anything else—a death blow at Rudolph I, Emperor of the Purple Empire, Master of Europe and Asia, and Conqueror of America.

Jimmy's lips tightened. He had not mentioned it to either MacPherson or Tim Donovan. But he had kept that purpose in mind when he had decided to go with Anita Monfred. Whether or not he learned about the pigeons, did not matter any more, for the big push must go on—rising or no rising. It could not be delayed any longer. But he had wanted just one chance to strike at Rudolph. And this might be the chance.

Anita Monfred indicated the service door. She tried the knob, pushed it open slightly. "See, it's unlocked, as I left it. And, you see, I told you the truth about it being unguarded. There was only a single sentry here, and he must be around on the other side, watching them put up the cage. Now the rest is up to you."

Jimmy Christopher nodded. "Thank you, Baroness," he said. "I want to apologize for suspecting you. And thank you for this chance. If I get Diane out of here, both of us will be grateful to you for the rest of our lives."

She lowered her eyes. "Do not thank me, Operator 5. I owe you this service. Perhaps, if we had been on the same side, our paths in life might have led more closely together. And now, you must go in quickly. Here I leave you. The rest is in your hands. Miss Elliot's cell is directly down the stairs, just inside this door. If you should meet anyone, your uniform will carry you past them. There is only one jailer in charge of Miss Elliot's cell, and there are no other prisoners there. You should have little difficulty there. When you release her, come straight back this way. You can mount the horses, and ride south. I wish you luck."

Jimmy Christopher bowed, and kissed the baroness's hand. "Thank you again," he whispered, and left her.

HE STEPPED through the delivery entrance, hand on holster, wary, alert. The corridor here was in utter darkness, and he flashed the beam of his pencil flashlight. It showed him the stairway leading down, just at the baroness had said. Swiftly, he closed the door behind him, and started down the stairs. His gun was out now, and he followed the beam of the flash. There had originally been storerooms here, but Rudolph had converted this portion of the building into detention cells for particular prisoners whom he did not wish kept with the others. It was only natural that Diane should be confined here.

Jimmy reached the bottom of the stairs, and located the cell door which Anita had told him he would find. There were five cells here, each provided with a thick oak door. Anita had said that Diane's was Number One. Jimmy saw it, and looked around for the jailer. He was nowhere in evidence.

Jimmy stepped swiftly to the door of Cell Number One. If the jailer had stepped out for a moment, it would save trouble.

He tried the door, found it locked as Anita had said it might be. She had said that the only way to open it would be to get the key from the jailer, or else to shoot the lock out. Jimmy wondered if the shots would be heard outside. He shrugged. He must chance it.

Leaning close to the door, he called, "Di! It's Jimmy. Stand away from the door—"

He paused, his blood chilling. From behind, a powerful flashlight suddenly bathed him in merciless glow. A cold voice said, "Stand very still, Operator 5!"

Jimmy Christopher's blood raced madly through his veins. He had been betrayed! Betrayed by the Baroness Anita Monfred! He had deliberately taken that chance, taken it with his eyes open. And he had lost!

Every nerve alert, every muscle taut, he prepared to whirl and shoot, to sell his life dearly.

And that cold voice behind him, as if reading his thoughts, said quickly, "Do not attempt to fight, Operator 5. It would be like tilting at a windmill. You are covered by three machine guns."

Jimmy Christopher grinned thinly. Better to be cut down by machine guns then to become a prisoner of the Emperor. He dropped to his knees, whirled, firing his revolver even as he turned.

Once, twice, three times he fired, expecting every moment to hear the deadly clatter of the machine guns, and to feel steel-jacketed slugs ripping through his flesh and his muscles, smashing his bones.

But no shots answered his fire!

He emptied his gun, switching his fire to the eye of the flashlight that was blinding him. He struck the light, throwing the place into darkness once more. Still, no shots answered him.

With his gun empty, he began to reload feverishly, puzzled that he was still alive. And, abruptly, another flashlight came to life. He saw now, bitterly, that it was being flashed at him from the aperture in the cell door opposite. And he saw, too, where his first shots had struck. He had been firing at the thick oak of one of the cell doors.

He was caught flat, with the unloaded gun still in his hand, when the cell door opposite opened to reveal the uniformed figure of Captain Kiel, the captain of the Guard. Beside him stood a trooper with a machine gun leveled at him.

Captain Kiel snapped an order, "Take him, men, alive!"

Immediately, the other cell doors opened, and troopers surged out, to surround him, to engulf him. They carried clubbed carbines, and they pressed about him, careful not to injure him. Jimmy Christopher, tight-lipped, clubbed his own revolver, and fought. He smashed at faces, at arms for a moment, and then he could fight no longer, for the troopers were pressing in close, pinioning his arms, holding him helpless.

The voice of the captain of the Guard came once more. "That is well, men." Then, "Operator 5, I call upon you to surrender. It is hopeless to resist further."

Jimmy Christopher, blinking into the flashlight, said bitterly: "Why ask me to surrender? It seems that I'm your prisoner. Give my regards to the Baroness Anita, and say to her that she did a good piece of work. No doubt the Emperor will give her one of my ears as a keepsake."

Captain Kiel stepped out from the cell. He shrugged deprecatingly.

"As one soldier to another, Operator 5," he said, "I wish to say that I admire you greatly. You were a gallant enemy, and it is a pity to have tricked you this way. I would rather have seen you go down fighting. But"—he spread his hands—"what would you? I have my orders, and they must be obeyed."

"No hard feelings, Captain," Jimmy said with a wry smile. "I deserve this. I should have known better than to trust that woman."

Captain Kiel bowed. "Your pardon for what I must do now. It is orders." He motioned with his hand, and the troopers seized Jimmy Christopher, tore the uniform tunic from him and the shirt underneath. In a moment he was stripped to the waist. Then they bound his hands behind him.

Jimmy Christopher offered no further resistance. He faced Captain Kiel, with his hands bound.

"Tell me one thing, Captain," he demanded. "Where is Miss Elliot?"

"She is in the courtyard. They are about to place her in the cage with the jaguar." He grimaced distastefully. "And it is the Emperor's orders that you be brought there as soon as you are captured, to witness the spectacle."

Jimmy felt a cold shiver surge through his body. He had been tricked, captured. Now he was to be compelled to watch while Diane was clawed to death by a jaguar.

For the first time, there was black despair in his heart as they led him up the stairs.

CHAPTER 9
TO BE TORN TO PIECES

CAPTAIN KIEL marched in advance, and an escort of six troopers kept closely bunched around Operator 5, as they moved through the wide corridors of the building, where a short year before the processes of free government had been administered by a duly elected governor—but where now only terror and cruelty stalked, under the guidance of an autocratic, vindictive Emperor.

The great building was in utter darkness, entirely deserted. For everyone had gone out into the courtyard to witness the spectacle being staged there by Rudolph. Captain Kiel used his flashlight to guide them out toward the front.

Here, Jimmy Christopher was led through the wide doorway to the throne chair where Rudolph I sat.

Jimmy threw a brief glance around the courtyard, saw the cage, glimpsed the jaguar stalking through it, and saw Diane, being led to the door of the cage by the troopers. Diane was not looking toward the dais, and did not see him. It was just as well, Jimmy thought.

The voice of Rudolph, sopping with gloating triumph, addressed him.

"At last you are my prisoner, Operator 5! Well, well! So the brave and clever Operator 5 was tricked by a woman! And when you die slowly, Operator 5, under the spiked ball of my good friend Balku, you can think of the way your sweetheart died before your eyes!"

110

Jimmy Christopher met the glance of Emperor Rudolph, and his look was full of scorn.

Rudolph was leaning forward in his seat, enjoying himself to the fullest. "Why don't you plead for your sweetheart's life, Operator 5? Perhaps you could move the Imperial heart to clemency? Perhaps there is some information you could give me, something you could do for me, that would influence me to spare her from that jaguar?" Jimmy Christopher glanced from Rudolph to Balku, who stood at the Emperor's left, smacking his thick lips; then he glanced at Baron Flexner, on the Emperor's right.

The baron squirmed under his level gaze, and dropped his eyes.

Jimmy smiled bitterly, and looked once more at Rudolph. "I see that you are surrounded by your rats, as usual. Don't you know, Rudolph, that the end is here? Don't you know that our troops are pushing forward at the Continental Divide while you waste your time here with these bestial cruelties? Don't you know that there are thirty thousand volunteers converging on Denver now? Don't you know that your bloody empire here in America is crumbling?"

He paused, watching Rudolph's face grow redder and redder. Then he went on, goadingly: "Ask you for mercy? It would be the same as asking that jaguar in the cage for mercy. Go on with your torture. Do everything that your vile mind can imagine. Tomorrow, you will no longer be an emperor, but a cheap, cowardly fugitive from the wrath of the avenging Americans!"

Rudolph had half risen in his seat, his face mottled with

fury. Gasps rose from the courtiers surrounding the Emperor,
at the audacity of such words, which no one had ever, in their
full remembrance, dared to utter in his presence. They all paled.

Rudolph got up from his chair, and trembling with fury he
raised a hand, brought it down hard across Operator 5's cheek.

He hurled the torch with full force.

He was mouthing hideous curses in his native language, trembling with rage and hate.

Baron Flexner did nothing to stop him. He understood the Emperor's rage very well, and he knew that Operator 5 had spoken as he did, through a keen knowledge of the Emperor's character.

Throughout the course of the Purple Invasion, only one man had loomed on the horizon as the inveterate enemy of the Emperor's rage, now so suddenly turned on. Time and again, Jimmy Christopher had tricked Rudolph, caused him to appear ridiculous to himself and his army. Only a short while ago, Operator 5 had very nearly succeeded in capturing the Emperor, and Rudolph had escaped by a hair, carrying a flesh wound from Operator 5's gun. Not only that, but the only woman whom Rudolph really cared for—Anita Monfred—had once been willing to forsake him for the American.

All these things had festered like sores on the soul of the Emperor, until his hate for Jimmy Christopher loomed above everything else. He had spent sleepless nights picturing what he would do to Operator 5 when he caught him, how he would make him cringe and beg.

And here, instead of fear, instead of pleas for mercy, he was confronted by a man unafraid, defiant—nay, by a man who threatened!

And it was too much for Rudolph. He gave way to ungovernable rage.

THE GUARDS at the door of the cage halted, astounded at the Emperor's transport. They kept their grip on Diane, but did not shove her in the cage as they had been about to do. The courtiers kept at a respectful distance, fearful lest the Emperor's rage be suddenly turned upon them. Even Balku hesitated to come near his master.

Only Baron Flexner dared. He was an old man now, and he had little left in life to fear. He came close to Rudolph, put a hand on his arm.

"Your Majesty! Compose yourself. Remember who you are! You are the Emperor! Do not show them that the Emperor can be goaded by one man!"

Rudolph suddenly sagged, his transport of rage leaving him as quickly as it had come. But as he seated himself in the chair once more, his small eyes rested upon Jimmy Christopher with such vindictiveness that Baron Flexner shuddered.

The Emperor watched Jimmy Christopher, and spoke out of the corner of his mouth to Balku. "You must do a good job on him, Balku. You must keep him alive for a week. A week, understand? I want him broken; I want him quivering; I want him begging and pleading. And I want to keep him that way for a week. If he dies before a week, I will have you flayed alive, Balku!"

The executioner bobbed his thick head. "I will keep him alive, master. Do not fear, you shall hear him scream yet."

"That is good!" Rudolph waved a hand. "Take him against the wall. Let him watch his sweetheart die!"

The guards seized Jimmy, dragged him back against one of the French windows that opened on the portico. They spread out, three guards on either side, as Rudolph waved to the troopers in charge of Diane.

The troopers bowed low, and one of them opened the door of the cage. The jaguar within growled, and pushed toward the open door. A man with one of the long poles thrust it at the jaguar, forcing the animal back from the opening. And Diane was pushed in. They slammed the door behind her, and she was left in the cage with the jaguar.

Jimmy Christopher could not tear his eyes from the scene. He wanted to do something, anything. He could not bear to stand this way and watch the animal tear Diane to shreds, as it would in a moment.

It was prowling around the cage now, all the way at the other end, sniffling the air, probably wondering what the presence of this woman meant. Suddenly, the animal stiffened, turned, and began to move toward her. It was stalking its prey just as it would do in the jungle.

And Jimmy Christopher almost groaned aloud at sight of Diane, standing slim and straight, with her back against the bars. DESPERATELY, HE glanced around the courtyard. Troopers were everywhere, drawn up in a cordon around the yard, as well as others posted at the far end. On the upper floor, Jimmy glimpsed the muzzles of two machine guns, protruding from the corner windows at each end of the building. That made it worse than ever now.

Rudolph was taking no chances on being caught off guard. Even though he might be enjoying himself at this spectacle, he had not forgotten that there was fighting in the city, and that there was a slim chance that the Americans might win through.

The picture of Rudolph, sitting there in his chair and watching Diane in the cage, while musketry boomed throughout the city, reminded Jimmy vividly of Nero fiddling while Rome burned. Time and again, he tore his eyes from Diane, to look around in search of some wild gamble that might free her. There was no hope in sight.

And now, the jaguar, sensing that this woman who had been thrust into its cage was defenseless, began to move slowly toward her. A deep hush descended upon the courtyard, making the distant shooting all the more audible.

Jimmy Christopher gnawed at his lower lip. In a matter of minutes, those claws would be tearing at Diane's soft body, lacerating it, gnashing it, opening great gouts through which her lifeblood would flow. And there was nothing—*nothing* that he could do!

Nothing?

Suddenly, a strange tension gripped Jimmy's frame. Cold sweat stood out on his brow. His ears had caught a slight noise which the guards had missed.

Somebody was opening the French window behind him!

No one in the Emperor's entourage would have to be so cautious in his movements. Jimmy tautened, every fiber alert. His eyes were still on Diane and the jaguar, but his ears were cocked for the slightest sound.

And it came. A hand touched his own bound hands. A thin voice whispered, "Jimmy! It's me—Tim!"

Tim Donovan! A sudden tingling gladness electrified Operator 5. He dared not talk, for fear of attracting the guards. He must leave everything to Tim's judgment. How the boy had come here he did not know. But he thanked God for the lad.

Tim was whispering again, "I had to follow you, Jimmy. I saw you go in there, and then I heard the woman laugh, so I knew she had double-crossed you."

Jimmy Christopher, listening to Tim and watching the cage at the same time, stirred impatiently. The jaguar was getting up courage to leap at Diane. It was hardly ten feet away, crouching, its mouth slavering. In a moment it would leap....

"I lost my gun running from some soldiers that wanted to stop me," Tim was whispering. "But I have my pen knife."

Jimmy Christopher felt a cool blade along his wrists, felt the knife severing the cords.

He was free!

But was he too late? The jaguar was about to leap!

Desperately, frantically, Jimmy leaped past the guard at his left, hurled himself at one of the torch-bearers. The guard uttered a shout, and the torch-bearer turned, startled.

Jimmy Christopher's knotted fist came up in a crashing blow to the man's jaw. He did not wait to see the man fall, but snatched the torch from his hand, whirled, and hurled it with full force toward the cage. He held his breath. Had he aimed well? There was so little space between those bars!

The torch spun through the air, and excited shouts went up from the spectators as it brushed lightly against one of the bars, then fell into the cage, directly in front of the jaguar! It sputtered, hissed.

The beast, like all felines, had an absorbing fear of fire. It was almost in the air when the torch fell. It reared back on its haunches, and leaped away from the flame.

Diane, her quick wits grasping the necessity of the moment,

stooped swiftly and picked up the torch, holding it so that the flame remained alive. She was safe for the moment.

But Jimmy Christopher had brought a hornet's nest down upon himself. The guards who had been assigned to watch him were stunned for a moment by his swift, lightning-like action. They knew that he had been securely bound; in fact they had put a couple of extra turns on the rope about his wrists, and had pulled it as tight as possible. The last thing in the world they expected was that he should get free.

They stood motionless for a second, as he flung the torch, not giving credence to the thing they were seeing. But instantly bewilderment was changed into rage and fear—rage at this captive who had literally snatched the torch from under their noses, and fear of the punishment that the Emperor would inflict upon them for their carelessness.

Uttering hoarse shouts, they flung themselves at Operator 5, while Rudolph, surrounded by his household guards, half rose in his chair shouting to them that if they let him escape he would flay them alive.

BUT JIMMY CHRISTOPHER was not taken off his guard this time, as he had been down in the cellar a little while ago. Even as he flung that torch he knew what his next move would be. He had an ace in the hole, which the enemy were not yet aware of—Tim Donovan. He was sure that the lad would have sense enough not to show himself, and he was right. Tim had remained discreetly hidden in the darkness behind the French window, after cutting Jimmy's bonds.

So now, Operator 5 whirled after flinging the torch, and

hurled himself bodily at the nearest trooper, the one who stood closest to the French window. The man was fumbling with his carbine, swinging it around so that he could use it as a club, for he remembered Captain Kiel's admonition to take Operator 5 alive.

Jimmy Christopher crashed past the clumsy fellow's carbine before he could lift it for a blow, and smashed a driving overhand left to the trooper's jaw. His knuckles cracked against jawbone, and the man went hurtling backward through the open French window, virtually into the arms of Tim Donovan, the carbine flying from his unconscious hands into the darkness of the room within.

Jimmy Christopher shouted, "Get that carbine, Tim!" and turned to meet the rush of the infuriated troopers. He had no chance against them, barehanded as he was. The troopers closed in on him, two of them darting around to block off his retreat through the French window.

One of them darted in at Jimmy with clubbed carbine, and Operator 5 dropped flat on the ground. The man's rifle butt swished through empty air, and he stumbled. The other troopers rushed in, and from the dark room inside came Tim's voice.

"I got it, Jimmy. Get down. Here it comes!"

Jimmy Christopher remained on the ground, and the carbine in Tim Donovan's hands barked once, twice, three times in quick succession. At this close range it was impossible for him to miss even if he'd been a poor shot. The two troopers, who were blocking Jimmy's retreat dropped with slugs through their faces, while

120

the one closest to him was suddenly hurled backward with a ball through his chest.

That was enough to demoralize the others. This attack, coming without warning from the dark interior of the building, was too much for them. They suddenly envisioned a company of Americans inside, about to mow them down, and they turned and fled precipitously.

Rudolph, surrounded by his household guards, shrieked to them to stand and fight, but his voice was drowned in the commotion. A Purple staff major near the Emperor's seat drew a revolver and aimed at Jimmy Christopher. But before he could fire, a shot from Tim Donovan's rifle caught him between the eyes.

Jimmy Christopher, still on his knees, reached out and seized the carbines and ammunition bandoleers of the two troopers whom Tim had shot. Bullets were cutting the pavement at his feet now, from the carbines of some of the troopers at the far end of the courtyard, who were emboldened to shoot by the fact that no swarm of Americans had come out of the building.

Jimmy gripped the two carbines, and leaped through the French window, almost colliding with Tim Donovan in the darkness. He seized the lad by the arm, dragged him to one side just as a hail of slugs poured in through the open window. Lead whipped into the floor past them, smashed into the far wall of the room, continued with a constant, crashing, drumming crescendo of noise, resounding shrilly in the confines of the chamber.

"Gosh, Jimmy," Tim Donovan shouted above the noise, "that was a close call! Let's get out of here!"

"Wait!" Jimmy ordered. "I want a shot at Rudolph!"

He stepped close to the wall, alongside the window, peered out toward the dais. His mouth drooped in a disappointed line. Rudolph was gone. The Emperor had not cared to remain in the open with all the shooting, and had moved inside at once, with his retinue.

JIMMY SEIZED Tim's arm, ran with him through a connecting door, into the next room, which also faced on the portico. The soldiers in the courtyard were concentrating upon the window they had left, and they were able to peer out through the window in this room without inviting shots. Jimmy Christopher saw that Diane was still in the cage, holding the torch as protection against the jaguar. At any moment now, one of the soldiers might take it into his head to shoot her. While she held that torch, she was an easy target. The rest of the courtyard was in darkness, for the torch-bearers had fled. Many of them had dropped their flaming torches, and these threw a fitful, shadowy light upon the figures of the troopers.

Jimmy Christopher pushed open the French doors, raised his rifle deliberately, and sighted at the jaguar. He fired a single shot, and the beast leaped high in the air, screeching, then dropped, an inert, lifeless mass. Jimmy fired another shot, plump into the lock on the door of the cage. The lock sagged, and the cage door slipped ajar.

Jimmy shouted, cupping his hands, "Di Di! Douse that torch. Drop to the floor!"

Diane heard him. Acting instantly, she reversed the torch and stamped it against the ground. The flame went out, leaving her shrouded in darkness. Jimmy sighed with relief.

He swung about in the darkness, gripped Tim Donovan by the shoulder. "Tim! I'm going to try to clear the square of soldiers. You wait down here. If I do it, you get out there, get Diane out of the cage, and make tracks for the south side of town. No arguments now"—as the boy started to protest—"we're working with split-seconds."

He thrust the extra carbine into the lad's hand. "Give this one to Diane." His hand tightened on Tim's arm, so that the youngster winced. "You must promise me to do what I've asked you. Quick, Tim—your promise!"

He spoke so fiercely, so urgently, that Tim said, "I—I promise, Jimmy."

"Good lad. Wait here now, till I clear the square."

"W-what are you going to do—" Tim broke off. He realized that Operator 5 had already slipped out of the room….

JIMMY CHRISTOPHER made his way into the corridor. He was still stripped to the waist, and he dared not be seen. He was sure that the building was being searched thoroughly for him. Luckily, no one was in this wing yet, and he found a staircase, mounted it rapidly. At the head of the stairs was a room with an open door. Jimmy peered inside, and nodded. He had found what he expected. When he stood bound, down below on the portico, he had seen the muzzle of a machine gun protruding from the window of the corner room, and he had come in search of it.

There was a single gunner in the room, and this man was peering out of the window at the shooting in the courtyard. He heard nothing until Jimmy was close to him, then he whirled, startled. He had a revolver in his hand, and his eyes opened wide as he saw and recognized Operator 5. Jimmy did not give him a chance to fire. He brought the carbine down on the fellow's head with a stunning blow.

The stock of the rifle split, and the man's skull was literally crushed in. He fell backward, his hand sending his revolver spinning out of the window with an involuntary jerk.

Jimmy Christopher threw away the useless carbine, stepped over the lifeless body to the machine gun at the window. The belt was in place, equipped with an automatic feeder, which rendered a second man unnecessary. The gun was a late-model Skoda, manufactured expressly for the Purple Empire. It was one of the models for which ammunition was becoming scarce. But there was enough in the belt for Jimmy's purpose.

He swung the gun about on its pivots to make sure it could be handled well, then peered out into the courtyard. The Purple troopers were still firing from the far end of the courtyard, and as Jimmy peered out, an officer raised his hand and the firing ceased. The officer barked a command, and the troopers fell into formation, then in a run toward the open French window below. They were charging.

Jimmy's lips compressed tightly, as his fingers manipulated the machine gun. This would be slaughter, but it was unavoidable. He would receive scant mercy from the Purple troops if he were caught again, and he had to clear the way for the escape of Diane and Tim.

He lowered the sights of the gun, pulled the trips, and held the deadly instrument steady while it bucked under his grip, vomiting forth a stream of tracer bullets. The hail of slugs swept down into the courtyard, cutting the pavement at the feet of the charging soldiers. They pulled up short, shouting with amazement and fear. They had not expected this. They had heard only one rifle from inside the building, and they thought they had only one or two men to contend with.

A machine gun was a far different matter. They were more accustomed to being on the sending rather than the receiving end of machine-gun fire.

They faltered, and would have retreated, but their officer's metallic voice, from behind the line, whipped them forward. Once more they advanced, and a couple of snipers raised their rifles to fire at Jimmy's window. Jimmy grimly raised his sights an inch, pulled the trip once more.

This time he had no compunctions. The hail of steel-jacketed bullets from his hot weapon plowed into the front ranks of those soldiers, mowing them down with deadly accuracy. Jimmy raked the line again and again, and the troopers dropped by the dozen. The second line pulled up short, raising their rifles, and Jimmy raised his sights slightly, let go again.

He swung the gun from left to right of that line, cutting the troopers down before they could fire.

This time it was too much for them. They broke, and ran in wild disorder toward the far end of the courtyard. Their officer ran with them, shouting commands. At the far end they halted, and the officer attempted to reform them.

Jimmy gave him no chance. He raised his sights two inches, prayed that he had gauged well, and pulled the trip. He caught the disordered troopers with the full blast of lead, dropping them so fast that they did not even have time to run. Those in the front rank all perished under the withering fire, and the others waited for nothing else. They turned and ran, this time not even stopping when they got outside the courtyard. Their officer was dead, and they had nothing to hold them.

These men knew that the penalty for running while under fire would be death at the hands of the executioner, so they did not remain, but disappeared into the night. Such incidents had occurred many times before in the Purple Army. Whole regiments had retreated under fire, and in order to avoid the wholesale executions which were sure to follow, they had disbanded and disappeared, to roam about the countryside, looting, pillaging and killing, until they were caught by the numerous Purple Empire patrols. This case was no different. By his very strictness, Rudolph had lost more than one company of soldiers.

And Jimmy Christopher sighed. It had been a difficult thing to do, this business of cutting down men by the dozen. But he had a picture always before him of raped, tortured, murdered women throughout America—victims of those very men who had been charging. And he had steeled himself to the job.

Now, comparative quiet abruptly descended upon the courtyard. Jimmy leaned far out of the window, and shouted down, "Get going, Tim!"

126

He watched for a moment, saw the small figure of Tim Donovan run out of the building, saw the figure of Diane Elliot come out to meet him. No one fired at the two of them from the building. No doubt everybody had kept away from the windows, in order to avoid being hit by a stray bullet. Thus, the very barrage of the Purple troops aided their victims to escape.

Jimmy Christopher watched grimly while Tim and Diane picked their way among the dead and dying, until they disappeared into the night.

Then he sighed. His job was still ahead of him. He meant to get Rudolph.

CHAPTER 10
CHARGE OF THE CONDEMNED

THERE WERE other men in Denver that night, whose minds were set upon the same goal which inspired Operator 5. In the streets of the city, MacPherson's Scouts, augmented by thousands of volunteers who had flocked in from every direction, were pushing slowly, at dreadful cost, along Cherry Creek toward the palace. They knew that Jimmy Christopher had ventured there as much for the purpose of seeking a chance to strike at Rudolph, as to rescue Diane Elliot; and though it was not expected of them, they were willing to make every sacrifice, to force the fighting so that they could be in at the crisis.*

---

* AUTHOR'S NOTE: It is significant of the esteem in which Operator 5 was held at this time by the rank and file of Americans, that they did not doubt

127

And indeed, in every other section of America, men were rising, flinging themselves desperately at well-armed, well-trained garrisons in every city in the land. At the front lines our men were pouring now across the enemy trenches, inspired by their victory, eager to reach Denver, to consolidate their gains before the Purple High Command could throw its powerful reserves into the breach in the lines.

But in Denver that night, the fighting was the most severe. Here, due to the presence of the Emperor, there was a stronger garrison than usual—and in addition, there were the two additional brigades of infantry. Nevertheless, Frank MacPherson, fighting in the barricades, side by side with his men, in spite of his lack of an arm, glowed with fierce joy as he blew three sharp

for a moment that his true purpose was the service of his country rather than the selfish one of rescuing the woman he loved. With any other man, there might have been the lingering doubt that he was going into danger for the sake of Diane. But they knew Operator 5 too well to think that he would have shrunk from entering the enemy lines with the Baroness Anita Monfred even if Diane Elliot had not been a prisoner of the Purple Emperor. In this connection it may be well to make note of the fate of Anita Monfred. Historians have advanced many conflicting theories on this subject. Even Harrison Stievers is rather vague on the point. The only thing known at this time, in spite of extensive research and questioning, is that Anita Monfred was seen walking toward the fighting in the southern part of the city, after performing her task of betrayal. That was the last that was ever seen of her. No man living today knows definitely what happened to her. She disappeared, on that night of the Denver Raid, and her fate has been a mystery ever since.

blasts upon his whistle in the signal to advance. He knew that his volunteers would push on, until the last breath was out of their bodies. If they were defeated here in the streets of the enemy capital tonight, it would not be for lack of courage!

His son, George, was fighting at his side, when the courier arrived from the reserve corps back in the concentration camp. The courier, sweating from his hard ride through the streets, pushed to the side of the MacPherson's, and reported swiftly.

"Captain Linster has flown in with a plane from the front lines, sir!" he reported. "He has landed in the concentration camp, and he wants to talk to you at once!"

Captain Linster was the officer assigned by Jimmy Christopher to take charge of the small force of planes at the disposal of the Americans at this time. There were hardly half a dozen of these machines now, and they were used mainly for scouting and observation, due to the lack of ammunition for their machine guns.

The MacPhersons' glanced at each other. If Linster wanted to talk with them, it must be important. He would not send for them this way, in the midst of the toughest battle of their lives, unless it were urgent. The mere fact that he had used a precious store of dwindling gasoline to fly in from the front indicated that his mission was of no little weight.

Rifles were crackling all about them, and ten feet away a desperate hand-to-hand mêlée was in progress where the Americans were striving to drive the enemy Uhlans out from behind a barricade of hastily torn-up paving-blocks.

Old Frank MacPherson motioned to his son. "You go see Linster, George. I've got to stay here with the boys."

George MacPherson nodded, and turned to follow the courier back toward the concentration camp. Five minutes later he was standing beside the small two-seater scout plane which Captain Linster had flown in.

He shook hands with the captain. "How's it going at the front?" he inquired anxiously.

Linster spoke quickly, jerkily, as if he had little time. "We're winning, George. They're on the run."

George MacPherson's eyes lighted up with relief. "Swell! And we'll hold up our end back here—"

Linster interrupted him. "Look here, Mac, I've got something for us to do. I flew in to establish a line of communication between Hank Sheridan and your dad. But that can wait. On the way in, I saw something that turned my stomach. You know where the enemy labor camp is located, over at Fort Collins?"

MacPherson nodded. "Yes. They've got almost a thousand men and women out there, working on the roads, and sewing for their troops."

"Well, I passed over Fort Collins on the way in. They've got those damned wooden crosses put up in the field, *and they've got our people strung up on those crosses for target practice!*"

George MacPherson paled. "They—they're going to shoot them all?"

Captain Linster's lips were tight, colorless. He had been a professor of English in Northwestern University before the

Purple Invasion, and he had dabbled in aeronautics as a hobby. Now he was in deadly earnest.

"I had no ammunition for the machine guns, but I had two bombs in the racks. I tried to release the bombs, but the mechanism is stuck. I've just had a couple of your boys look at it, and they say it can't be fixed. But we've got to do something, Mac. We can't let them shoot all those people!"

George MacPherson's eyes became bleak. "We'll do something all right. How many troops have they got there?"

"I didn't see more than a hundred altogether. They looked like they were going to have a regular party in the field there—a sort of gunnery contest, with live targets!"

George said, "Wait a second, Linster!"

He shouted to the men who had gathered around them, "Anybody got a sub-machine gun?"

The men spread out through the camp, spreading the word that a sub-machine gun was wanted. In a moment, one of the men came running toward them, carrying the required weapon.

The man grinned. "I found it in the barracks building, Mac. It's fully loaded, but there's only the one clip. It's good for a single spray, and no more."

Mac nodded. "That'll have to do." He swung to Linster. "Let's go, Cap!"

Linster said dryly, "Better put on a parachute, Mac. I think we may need to bail out before we're through. I've got an extra one for you."

MacPherson put it on, and climbed into the observer's seat, while Linster took the throttle. He had left the engines running, and in a moment they were speeding across the clearing in a perfect take-off.

LINSTER CLIMBED to two thousand feet, then leveled off. Below them they could see the panorama of Denver, with small black, ant-like figures swarming in frantic motion everywhere in the darkness, appearing a strange, livid hue under the lights of the numerous torches.

Captain Linster pointed to the bomb-rack mechanism, and shrugged his shoulders. He spoke into the inter-cockpit phone. "If the worst comes to the worst, I'll dive into those fiends, and blow them to hell!"

George MacPherson nodded, in silence.

It was almost no time before they were over Fort Collins. And George, looking over the side, saw that Linster had told the truth. The scene that spread below them in the night was one that could chill the blood of the strongest man.

A broad field, perhaps an acre in size, lay just to the north of the detention buildings which served as the quarters for the forced labor corps of drafted Americans.

At one end of this field, a long row of black crosses had been erected, and upon each of these crosses was tied a man or a woman. At the other end of the field, the enemy troops, about a hundred strong, were drawn up in small squads of four. They stood at attention, all except one squad at the end of the line. This squad had rifles at their shoulders, aiming at the first batch of victims upon the crosses.

George MacPherson felt the blood racing through his frame. He tapped Linster on the shoulder, and the captain looked down, banked toward the field. Even as they both watched, a Purple officer at the end of the field raised his hand, and the four rifles of the kneeling squad barked.

MacPherson and Linster could not hear the shots, because of the droning of their motors. But they could see the small plumes of smoke from the rifles, and in the fitful flare of the torchlights they could see the first four figures on the crosses jerk with the impact of the bullets, and then slump.

George MacPherson could not restrain a cry of agony. They were shooting them down four at a time; they were going to make a night's sport of it, while war waged everywhere around, while Americans fought for life and liberty. They were killing these people for target practice!

Captain Linster motioned to George to get his machine gun ready. The two men were grim-lipped as Linster pushed the stick forward, and dived toward the line of troopers. It was a crazy, foolhardy thing to do, and both men knew it. But they could already see the second group of troopers kneeling, awaiting the signal to fire. And they thought of nothing but stopping that carnage.

The troopers had seen the plane by this time, but they paid it little attention, thinking perhaps, that it was one of their own machines. In any event they would not be unduly worried, as it was well known to the enemy that the American crates had no ammunition for the guns.

Linster and MacPherson kept their cold eyes on that line of mass executioners as the ground hurtled up to meet them in their mad dive. MacPherson raised his sub-machine gun to his shoulder, waited until the plane was so low that they could see the faces of the Uhlans, illuminated by the flares. Then he let go, sent a spray of lead into the heart of the line. Troopers stumbled under his blast, and the line broke. MacPherson kept his finger on the trip for a full half minute, while Linster brought the plane almost down to the ground; then he had to let up, for Linster pulled the ship sharply out of its dive, in order to rise and come down for a second blast.

Some of the troopers were running, others had dropped to the ground, while a few, at the far end of the line, had raised their rifles and were peppering the plane.

Wind screamed in the struts as Linster pulled the ship out of her dive. Black holes appeared in the wings, where the rifle fire from the ground struck. Linster kept the ship in her steady climb, and for a moment MacPherson did not understand why he failed to bank and dive again. The ground was swiftly receding as he looked over the side. He tapped the pilot on the shoulder, intending to motion him down again.

But when Linster turned around, MacPherson saw the tautness of his face, and knew at once that something was wrong. A chill swept through him as he turned his head to follow the pilot's arm. And his eyes widened as he saw the thick spume of billowing smoke, flecked with flame, that shaped a streaking tail in the rear of their plane.

The crate was afire!

A lucky bullet from one of the enemy rifles must have struck a vital spot, he thought. He had expected it, but the reality was worse than the anticipation in this case. He had never been in a burning plane before. He met the gaze of Captain Linster, who had turned around to look at him. Both men smiled, wanly. Then, almost as if by instinct, their hands met in a hard, tight clasp. Linster kept the ship climbing with one hand, while he gripped MacPherson's hand. His lips formed words.

"Bail out, Mac. Good luck!"

Without asking, George MacPherson knew what Linster intended to do. And he knew, too, what he, himself, intended to do.

He stood up in his seat, unstrapping the safety-belt. He gripped the sub-machine gun under his arm, waved to Linster, and waited while the captain leveled out. Then he jumped over the side, into space.

THE PLANE was blazing now, and Linster kept pushing her to the limit to keep the fire behind, as he circled the field, watching MacPherson. He saw MacPherson drop, plummet-like, until the parachute strapped to his back billowed out, stopping his fall with a jerk.

Linster kept the burning plane high, while Mac dropped, jerking at the lines of the parachute to bring him over the field. Down below, the troopers had formed their lines anew, and they were kneeling with raised rifles, waiting for MacPherson to descend close enough for good shooting.

Linster's mouth was a thin, tight line as he flew his blazing ship instinctively, and watched the scene below. At last he saw MacPherson close to the ground, saw the spurts of flame from the tracer bullets of his sub-machine gun. MacPherson was actually firing at those troops!

They burst in with the wild fury of an unleashed tornado, scattering

the blood-maddened men of the Emperor, right and left.

The Uhlans below answered his fire, neglecting the figures on the crosses at the other end of the field, for this new sport of shooting at a man on a parachute. Linster saw a dozen Uhlans fall, before the sub-machine dropped from the lifeless fingers of Mac's bullet-riddled body. George MacPherson had taken his quota of the enemy with him into his own death.

Now, the parachute reached the ground, and the eager, triumphant troopers ran toward the crumpled, lifeless body under the parachute. And Linster's eyes lighted with hot fire. Now was *his* chance.

He uttered a short prayer, glanced behind to look at the flames, then pushed the stick forward, all the way!

The plane answered his last summons, went into a terrible power dive that threatened to tear every strut from the frame. But Linster did not care. He wanted to get down—*fast*.

And get down he did. The amazed troopers did not have a chance to run. At one moment, they saw the burning crate screaming down toward them, and at the next it had struck among them.

The two bombs in the rack exploded with a detonation that shook the crosses at the other end of the field. High-powered explosive, designed to spread death for a hundred yards in every direction, that explosion tore a hole in the face of the earth that literally swallowed up the eager, triumphant Uhlans. Smoke, black and grisly, mingled with the flames that poured upward as from a burning oil-well. Not a man of those troopers escaped destruction.

And almost as an echo of that explosion, there came to the

ears of the deafened victims on the crosses, the beat of American drums, and shrill fifes playing *Yankee Doodle.* The Americans were arriving! The first wave had pushed on past the enemy tranches toward Denver, and the vanguard reached that field in time to witness the spectacle of a blazing funeral pyre, in which the names of two gallant men were forever to be burned into the scroll of American history.

AND WHILE MacPherson and Linster were gladly giving their lives to save their countrymen, Operator 5 was fighting his own battle, looking at the far-off city toward the dark, imposing crests of the Continental Divide, where Hank Sheridan and the American Defense Force would be fighting it out hot and hard with the might of Kremer's crack divisions. Zero hour was past. They had gone over the top. How were the boys doing? There was no way for him to learn. He could only pursue his course here, and hope that the big push would go over.

He turned from the window, surveyed the room in search of a weapon. There was none. But his eyes did light on a recessed door at the left. Outside in the corridor, he heard running feet. They would know, of course, that it was he who had operated the machine gun, and they were coming to get him. The corridor door was open, and he heard low shouts, crisp commands. This time they would shoot first. He could not afford to go out into that corridor.

Once more his glance shifted to the recessed door. That was his only chance. Where it led to, he could not tell. But it was the route he had to take.

Swiftly, he ran across the room, tried the door. It opened to his touch. The running troopers in the hall were only a few paces from the room now, and Jimmy Christopher did not hesitate. He slipped through, pulled the door shut behind him. He was in utter darkness.

His fingers, sliding along the edge of the door, found a bolt, and he shot it home. And then he heard loud voices through the door, in the room he had just quit.

Some one exclaimed, "He's been here and gone. Let's search this wing!"

They had not noticed, or had not thought of, the recessed door!

Quietly, Jimmy Christopher stole down the stairs, feeling his way in the darkness. It was cold here, and the clamminess seemed to cling to his naked torso. He went down a whole flight of stairs, slowly, groping in the dark. There was a bend in the stairs, and he took it. He came up against a closed door, tried it, and found that it opened.

He pushed it ajar, and suddenly his eyes blazed. He was standing in the doorway of the torture chamber where Rudolph and Balku had wrung the information as to Diane Elliot's whereabouts from the lips of Randall's wife. He did not know of that incident, but he knew the nature of the chamber, for there, in a far corner, stood the rack upon which they had tortured Joseph Randall.

They had moved it out of the center of the room, close to the wall where the cell doors were located. But Randall still hung upon the rack. And before Randall stood the thick, barrel-chested figure of Balku.

Balku was laughing in glee, as he playfully tapped Randall's bare chest with his heavy spiked ball. Just as Jimmy stepped into the room, Balku was raising his gruesome torture instrument for another blow. This sadistic fiend was not troubled by the fighting in the city, or by the fact that two important prisoners of the Emperor had just escaped. All he wanted was the pleasure of inflicting torture. And while all the household guards were searching the building for Operator 5, Balku had come down here to finish the work he had begun upon Randall earlier in the day!

Randall was a strong man, and he was still fully conscious. His eyes were wide open, and he saw Jimmy Christopher. Something in his attitude must have warned Balku, for the executioner whirled about, stopped aghast at sight of Jimmy Christopher.

Suddenly, his mouth opened in a deep, roaring laugh, as he saw that Jimmy was unarmed.

Jimmy Christopher's fingers were itching to get at the executioner's throat. He saw the tortured body of Randall, and he wanted to pay the bloody fiend for it. He forgot he was not armed, and launched himself at Balku. He was fighting mad.

THE EXECUTIONER, who had expected Jimmy to cringe before his swinging club, was momentarily paralyzed with fear. Bravery, audacity, recklessness of life, had always remained something of a black miracle to the followers of the Purple Emperor. Nurtured in an atmosphere of fear and terror and fawning sycophantism, they could never understand the courage that can place honor above life. So that when Jimmy Christopher came at him, unarmed, the man became panicky.

Instead of meeting the attack with his club, he raised the torture instrument above his head, and hurled it straight at Jimmy's face.

Jimmy Christopher saw the motion, telegraphed by Balku's clumsy movements. He lowered his head, dived in at the man. And the heavy iron club hurtled through the air, over his head, to smash up against the far wall with a dull clang.

Jimmy Christopher's tackle carried Balku backward, throwing him off balance, sending him to the ground. Jimmy twisted free of the executioner's wildly clutching hands. He smashed blow after blow to the other's face and head, and Balku, the Executioner, the man who had tortured thousands, who had laughed at the pain and the agony he had inflicted upon others, screamed for mercy.

Jimmy seized a saber, lying on the floor, and held him at bay.

"Stop, stop! Mercy!" Balku shouted, his voice rising in a queer screech that reechoed from the vaulted ceiling like the wail of some vile denizen of the underworld.

But Jimmy Christopher dared not leave him here. He had more work to do, and he did not wish to be taken in the rear. Deliberately, Jimmy hauled the man up by the leather jacket he wore, and stood him upon his two feet. Balku cringed away, but Jimmy Christopher stepped in, raised a smashing uppercut to the side of his jaw. There was a crackling sound, a snapping of bone. Balku screamed once; the scream changed into a gurgle, and he collapsed to the floor, unconscious from the pain of his broken jaw.

Jimmy stood over him for a moment, rubbing his knuckles. Then he looked up, to see Randall staring at him from the rack.

"Man!" Randall exclaimed. "That was a giant's blow! Chalk one up for you!"

He had never met Jimmy before, and did not know him. Jimmy knelt beside Balku's body, found a ring of keys, and a jack-knife. With the knife, he cut the bonds that held Randall to the rack. As he cut, he spoke swiftly, telling Randall who he was, what he wanted to do.

When Randall was free, he sagged for a moment, and Jimmy had to support him. But almost at once he straightened. "I'm all right, Operator 5. And if you want any recruits for the job, there's about forty men in those cells that would give their immortal souls for a chance at Rudolph!"

Jimmy's eyes gleamed. "Come on, then! What are we waiting for?"

With Randall at his side he hurried from cell to cell, unlocking doors. Within a few short minutes, forty-four men stood in that chamber—gaunt men, lean, hungry, emaciated, wounded and dirty, but every one of them with a hard, daring gleam in his eye. Silently, they listened to Jimmy, who spoke rapidly, passionately.

He finished up his short harangue. "And so, boys, if you want to get at Rudolph, here's your chance! You have no weapons. It'll be bare hands against guns and swords. But—"

"Let's go!" they shouted, interrupting him.

Jimmy Christopher smiled at them. "How can we lose?" he asked softly.

He turned and led the way swiftly across the chamber, not up the staircase by which he had descended, but along the main stairs, leading to the center of the building. On the way, he stooped and picked up the spiked club from the floor where it had fallen. The men thronged after him, silent, but eager.

They passed a storeroom, and Randall, who was close beside him, said, "Wait, Operator 5. There are weapons in here. I've seen officers come and go from this room."

Jimmy Christopher tried the door. It was locked. He raised his spiked club, smashed it against the door, and the wood gave. He broke out a panel, reached in and opened the door. It was the armorer's room. Randall grinned, eyeing the racks of swords against the walls.

"This is where the dandy court officers get their blades tuned up. It'll be a joke to slit their throats with their own swords!"

With a shout of joy the men rushed to the walls, seizing swords, sabers, rapiers. Some took two.

Jimmy Christopher provided himself with a serviceable-looking blade, and swished it through the air. He was an expert swordsman, having studied for more than two years, as a stripling, with the greatest masters of Europe and the Orient. He knew a good blade when he saw one, and this would serve his purpose well.

"Come on, boys!" he shouted, and led the way from the room. **THE TROOP** was a strange, macabre looking one as it followed Operator 5 up the board stairs into the main corridor. As they ascended, the sounds of shooting came closer and closer, pounding at their ears. There was fighting going on close outside the building.

The main corridor was crowded with courtiers, and a few officers, all standing near the broad arched doorway of the Emperor's audience chamber. They were peering in, but when they saw the motley crowd, led by the half-naked Jimmy Christopher, they gasped, and backed away.

A few more hardy souls raised pistols or attempted to draw swords. But Jimmy's men swarmed upon them so fast that they had no opportunity to fight. They were cut down ruthlessly, the men from the cells fighting with all the mad venom that weeks and months in the dark dungeons had instilled in them. They burst in with the wild fury of an unleashed tornado. They pushed through the throng at the doorway of the audience chamber, scattering it like chaff, and stormed into the room, uttering wild shouts that echoed above the noises of musketry in the streets outside.

Jimmy Christopher, in the lead, saw that the room was crowded with household guards, Imperial officers, and a small group of staff officers around the dais where Rudolph I sat.

Rudolph leaped from his seat, clawing at the sword at his side, and the staff officers swiftly grouped themselves about him on the dais to protect him from revolver shots with their own bodies.

The main group of Jimmy's men raised their voices in wild shouts, and charged into the room, slashing away madly with their swords, engaging the household guards. The room at once became a bedlam of clashing swords, shuffling feet, foul oaths in many languages, groans of the dying and shrieks of the wounded.

Jimmy Christopher never lost sight of his objective. He fended off attacks, not even bothering to reply to a thrust from a petty Purple officer. Resolutely, with but one purpose in mind, he made his way toward the dais.

There, the staff officers were formed into a living shield about their Emperor, standing with drawn swords. A few of the Americans from cells were pecking at them with sword thrusts, but these officers were skillful swordsmen, and had little difficulty in driving the Americans back.

Jimmy Christopher hit that living shield like an avalanche. There were four or five of the staff officers, and they all swung to face Operator 5. Jimmy laughed aloud, and leaped up that dais, his blade singing in the air, darting in and out with the speed of lightning and the elusiveness of a serpent.

He parried a thrust, ran a man through, almost in the same motion, and then his blade whirled before the eyes of the officers, engaging one, two, three at a time. He never gave back a single step, but kept pushing up all the time, slowly, inexorably. A second and a third man fell to his sword point, while the battle in the room raged all about them.

And then, suddenly, there was no one left between him and the Emperor. The way was clear at last!

RUDOLPH HAD his sword out, his back to the throne. He was snarling like a cornered beast. He had seen Operator 5 dispose of his most skilled swordsmen, and he was frightened. His soldiers were fighting all about him in the room, but none

Jimmy Christopher lowered his head, dived in at the man.

came to his assistance; they were all fighting for their own lives now.

Operator 5 advanced slowly, his sword-point level with his eyes, his gaze steady upon the Emperor.

Rudolph watched him with fascinated eyes. And, suddenly, he uttered a little cry of panic, and lowered his sword. His face was ashen.

"Don't kill me!" he muttered. "I—I yield!"

Jimmy Christopher's eyes burned with frustration. He had looked forward to the moment when he could run his sword through this vile being who had conquered the whole world, but not his own passions or appetites. And now he was to be cheated of that pleasure. It was a shame.

He shrugged. "Drop your sword!" he snapped.

Rudolph threw a single desperate glance at the fight in the room, but there was not a soul to whom he could appeal for aid. He gulped, and threw down his blade.

Jimmy raised his voice, so that all in the room could hear him.

"Rudolph, the First," he called out stertorously, "in the name of the American Republic, I arrest you!"

His voice, rising above the turmoil of the conflict, impinged upon the ears of the fighting Purple officers like the knell of doom. There was a sudden lull in the battle, and all eyes were turned toward the dais, where they saw the dejected figure of the once grandiose Rudolph, almost cringing before the naked blade of Operator 5.

That sight completed the demoralization of the Purple officers. Almost with one accord, they threw down their arms, clamoring to surrender. What was the use of fighting for a cause that was no longer a cause? What was the use of fighting for an Emperor who was a prisoner of the enemy? How could he reward or punish them?

Jimmy Christopher's men raised loud shouts of victory, and the news spread like wildfire out through the corridor, and into the courtyard, thence to the streets where the fighting was going on close to the palace now.

"Rudolph has surrendered! Rudolph has surrendered!"

Perhaps in less time than it takes to tell it, the Purple troops quit the fight. They threw down their arms indiscriminately, either begging for quarter, or fleeing into the night.

And ten minutes later, Frank MacPherson stalked into the audience chamber at the head of his scouts, to shake the hand of Operator 5.

The one-armed scout leader threw a contemptuous glance at Rudolph, who stood mutely, a prisoner of two husky Americans. Then he swung to Jimmy Christopher. "You've done it, Operator 5!" he shouted. "You've done it!"

Tim Donovan and Diane Elliot came up behind MacPherson, and Jimmy spied them. They both came into his arms at once. Diane said nothing. Her lips were trembling.

Jimmy stroked her hair, and her near-hysteria subsided.

"Jimmy!" she said throatily. "Is it true? Is the war over? Can we be together again, and not have to risk our lives every day any more? Can I love you without the specter of war on the threshold?"

He kissed her. "I hope so, darling."

Tim Donovan wriggled out from between them. "All right," he sulked. "Go ahead and have a love scene, you two!"

Jimmy laughed, and mussed his hair. Frank MacPherson drew him aside. "I picked up a heliograph from Hank Sheridan," he said. "Hank reports that the American Defense Force has smashed through the Purple Armies. They're marching across the country. The cavalry is mopping up ahead of them, and should be in Denver soon." His eyes sparkled.

Jimmy Christopher sighed. "It's about time. A little peace—"

Frank MacPherson smiled sadly, shaking his head in the negative. "I'm afraid we won't have peace, Operator 5. There's plenty of work ahead—tough, grueling work; and it may be even worse than the war has been."

"What do mean?" Jimmy demanded.

"There's another heliograph come in, relayed from New York. The uprisings took place all over the country, as planned. The Purple troops have been routed almost everywhere, but they've taken to the hills, and gone into the deserts and the open country. They'll be a menace to us until they're cleaned up—and we've a heavy job of reconstruction ahead, without that!"

Jimmy Christopher stared into space, his features set grimly.

"We'll face it, Mac, the way we've faced the Purple Invasion. You've seen how Americans can fight, against enormous odds. We'll lick that problem, the way we licked the Purple Empire. America just *can't* be destroyed!"

"God grant that you're right, Operator 5!" Frank MacPherson said solemnly.*

---

* AUTHOR'S NOTE: With Rudolph I a prisoner, America once more had a chance to catch her breath and take stock. She found all her manufacturing facilities destroyed, her natural resources destroyed and depleted in many cases. Guerrilla bands of ex-Purple soldiers roved the country, burning and pillaging, setting up small autocracies of their own in outlying districts, whence they could conduct bloody raids upon our settlements. This phase, prosaically termed "The Post Invasion Reconstruction Period," was in reality crammed with hairbreadth adventure and deadly peril, will be related in the next novel in this series.

POPULAR HERO PULPS AVAILABLE NOW:

THE SPIDER

❏ #1: The Spider Strikes	$13.95
❏ #2: The Wheel of Death	$13.95
❏ #3: Wings of the Black Death	$13.95
❏ #4: City of Flaming Shadows	$13.95
❏ #5: Empire of Doom!	$13.95
❏ #6: Citadel of Hell	$13.95
❏ #7: The Serpent of Destruction	$13.95
❏ #8: The Mad Horde	$13.95
❏ #9: Satan's Death Blast	$13.95
❏ #10: The Corpse Cargo	$13.95
❏ #11: Prince of the Red Looters	$13.95
❏ #12: Reign of the Silver Terror	$13.95
❏ #13: Builders of the Dark Empire	$13.95
❏ #14: Death's Crimson Juggernaut	$13.95
❏ #15: The Red Death Rain	$13.95
❏ #16: The City Destroyer	$13.95
❏ #17: The Pain Emperor	$13.95
❏ #18: The Flame Master	$13.95
❏ #19: Slaves of the Crime Master	$13.95
❏ #20: Reign of the Death Fiddler	$13.95
❏ #21: Hordes of the Red Butcher	$13.95
❏ #22: Dragon Lord of the Underworld	$13.95
❏ #23: Master of the Death-Madness	$13.95
❏ #24: King of the Red Killers	$13.95
❏ #25: Overlord of the Damned	$13.95
❏ #26: Death Reign of the Vampire King	$13.95
❏ #27: Emperor of the Yellow Death	$13.95
❏ #28: The Mayor of Hell	$13.95
❏ #29: Slaves of the Murder Syndicate	$13.95
❏ #30: Green Globes of Death	$13.95
❏ #31: The Cholera King	$13.95
❏ #32: Slaves of the Dragon	$13.95
❏ #33: Legions of Madness	$12.95
❏ #34: Laboratory of the Damned	$12.95
❏ #35: Satan's Sightless Legion	$12.95
❏ #36: The Coming of the Terror	$12.95
❏ #37: The Devil's Death-Dwarfs	$12.95
❏ #38: City of Dreadful Night	$12.95
❏ #39: Reign of the Snake Men	$12.95
❏ #40: Dictator of the Damned	$12.95
❏ #41: The Mill-Town Massacres	$12.95
❏ #42: Satan's Workshop	$12.95
❏ #43: Scourge of the Yellow Fangs	$12.95
❏ #44: The Devil's Pawnbroker	$12.95

❏ #45: Voyage of the Coffin Ship	$12.95
❏ #46: The Man Who Ruled in Hell	$13.95
❏ #47: Slaves of the Black Monarch	$13.95
❏ #48: Machineguns Over the White House	$13.95
❏ #49: The City That Dared Not Eat	$13.95
❏ #50: Master of the Flaming Horde	$13.95
❏ #51: Satan's Switchboard	$13.95
❏ #52: Legions of the Accursed Light	$13.95
❏ #53: The City of Lost Men	$13.95
❏ #54: The Grey Horde Creeps	$13.95
❏ #55: City of Whispering Death	$13.95
❏ #56: When Thousands Slept in Hell	$13.95
❏ #57: Satan's Shakles	$14.95
❏ #58: The Emperor From Hell	$14.95
❏ #59: The Devil's Candlesticks	$14.95
❏ #60: The City That Paid to Die	$14.95
❏ #61: The Spider at Bay	$14.95
❏ #62: Scourge of the Black Legions	$14.95
❏ **NEW**: #63: The Withering Death	$14.95

THE WESTERN RAIDER

❏ #1: Guns of the Damned	$13.95
❏ #2: The Hawk Rides Back from Death	$13.95
❏ #3: Gun-Call for the Lost Legion	$13.95
❏ #4: The Law of Silver Trent	$13.95
❏ #5: The Gun-Prayer of Silver Trent	$13.95
❏ #6: Silver Trent Rides Alone	$13.95

G-8 AND HIS BATTLE ACES

❏ #1: The Bat Staffel	$13.95

CAPTAIN SATAN

❏ #1: The Mask of the Damned	$13.95
❏ #2: Parole for the Dead	$13.95
❏ #3: The Dead Man Express	$13.95
❏ #4: A Ghost Rides the Dawn	$13.95
❏ #5: The Ambassador From Hell	$13.95

DR. YEN SIN

❏ #1: Mystery of the Dragon's Shadow	$12.95
❏ #2: Mystery of the Golden Skull	$12.95
❏ #3: Mystery of the Singing Mummies	$12.95